Whispers of Rain

The Orion Dynasty Book 3

CK Franco

Blurbs

He saved lives with steady hands—
until one mistake shattered him.
I was never meant to be his cure.

Dr. Darius Hale is the surgeon the world calls perfect—until one night breaks him. Lila Moreno is the nurse who sees past his armor, the only one brave enough to whisper hope into his silence.

But in a hospital ruled by power, politics, and the Brotherhood's shadow, love is the one risk that could cost them everything.

Broken hero. Redemption. A forbidden desire that could either heal—or destroy.

*For those who have ever carried grief in silence,
for the healers who break while mending others,
for the souls who learned to breathe again through the storm—
this story is for you.
May Darius's rain remind you that tears are not weakness,
but proof that you dared to love,
and proof that you still can.*

"The rain does not ask if we are ready;
it falls to cleanse what we can no longer hold."

Prologue

The operating room was a sanctuary of precision, where seconds were lifetimes and mistakes carved themselves into memory. For Dr. Darius Hale, it had once been holy ground—the place where his steady hands defied fate and rewrote endings.

Until the night he couldn't.

The monitors went silent. The team's voices blurred. And beneath the sterile lights, something inside him fractured in a way no scalpel could repair. From that night forward, he became a man bound by shadows—a surgeon with a perfect reputation, but a hollow chest. Cold. Controlled. Untouchable.

And then, the rain came.

Not from the sky, but from a woman who refused to look away. She was not a patient, not a colleague, not part of his world at all—yet her quiet strength became the storm that stirred his silence. She saw the cracks no one else dared to notice. She heard the whispers in his midnight hours.

He told himself she was danger.

He told himself she was impossible.

But the truth was written in every heartbeat he tried to deny:

Sometimes, the only way to heal is to let yourself break.

And sometimes, the whispers in the rain are not of grief—

but of love, waiting to be found.

Contents

1. The Operating Room Silence   1

2. Nurse on the Night Shift   11

3. First Collision   19

4. Cracks in Perfection   26

5. Unwanted Concern   33

6. Rain Against Glass   41

7. The Walls He Builds   48

8. Lila's Burdens   55

9. A Fracture in the Ice   65

10. Stolen Breaks   74

11. The Rumor Mill   84

12. An Unexpected Rescue   92

13. The Kiss in the Stairwell   99

14. Hospital Politics   107

15.	Betrayal in White Coats	118
16.	The Choice to Stay	128
17.	Confession Under Rain	137
18.	Love Exposed	147
19.	Sacrifice	156
20.	Whispers of Rain	167
	Epilogue	177
	Final Thoughts	179
	Review Request	180

The Operating Room Silence

The operating room is quiet and cold as Darius Hale stands over the patient. The metal counters shine under the hospital lights, sharp and clean. He reads the chart carefully, checking every vital sign and note—he can't trust his memory alone. The bright surgical lights illuminate his gloved hands clearly. He feels confident. This is where he is in control, where everything must be exact—there is no room for mistakes.

"Scalpel," he says calmly.

The nurse hands him the tool, her breathing shallow as the ventilator hums nearby. The smell of antiseptic mixes with the faint scent of blood and tension. Darius makes the first cut, feeling the skin give way under his hand, a sensation he knows well. In this room, every move follows a routine—everyone watches him, and his reputation depends on it. He leads the team, or at least that's what he tells himself.

But beneath his calm, a deep fear beats inside. To fail here is more than just a human mistake; it would break his reputation and betray the Brotherhood's strict code of silence.

Blood flows where it shouldn't. Darius frowns and changes his grip without stopping.

"There's unexpected bleeding. Get the retractors," he speaks sharply. The heart monitor beeps steadily, but tension rises.

The anesthesiologist nods and prepares injections. The nurse tightens her voice: "Pressors ready." (Pressors are medications that raise blood pressure.)

"Clamp it now. Suction." Surgical tools are passed to him quickly, wet with disinfectant. He looks for the source—a hidden blood vessel that didn't show up on scans or the chart. Time feels heavy. Everyone in the room watches him closely, waiting for him to fail.

The junior doctor's hands shake. The clamp slips. Blood spreads, soaking the drapes. The monitor's beep changes.

"Focus," Darius says coldly. Sweat drips down his neck. He stays steady, keeping his voice firm.

"Put in another stitch. We're losing pressure." He works faster, giving orders, trying to regain control. His breath fogs his mask.

The heart monitor beeps faster. The team's tension is like a tight wire ready to snap. Tools collide; sterile pads soak up blood but never enough. The room smells sharp, and the air feels thick with panic.

"Give a bolus. Ready the paddles," he commands. The resident's hands shake, but another nurse steadies him silently. Darius acts from memory and instinct, focused and sharp.

Still, the patient's condition worsens. The heart monitor line becomes erratic.

"Come on, again," Darius tightens his jaw. "Squeeze the bag. Where's the second unit of blood?"

His own heart pounds unevenly—a secret weakness that could break his composed image. Despite his skill, the patient's condition continues to decline. The monitor's beep fades.

A flatline sound blares.

Time seems to stop.

He removes his hands, his voice empty. "Time of death: 02:41." The words feel heavy. His voice is steady, but inside he feels like he is falling. The team steps back, tired, relieved but cold. Faces are sweaty and shadowed behind masks. They have lost.

In a corner, two nurses whisper with hunched shoulders, glancing to see if he notices. The junior doctor looks down, his lashes shaking, wishing to disappear. Another worker writes quickly on forms, trying to make sense of what happened.

The air is thick with antiseptic and an invisible pressure that squeezes the chest. Darius takes off his gloves; they snap loudly. His hands look pale. The bright lights, once comforting, now feel harsh, making him seem like a ghost, drained of certainty.

His chest tightens; he wants to breathe deeply to break free from guilt and the heavy silence around him. But he stands still. He cannot show the pain behind his eyes or how close he feels to breaking.

Around him, the hospital gears up for routine and rumors—the beginning of how private failure becomes public danger. At St. Gabriel's, every mistake stirs unseen forces. One death can cause chaos, disturb power, and break secret deals. The Brotherhood demands perfection. There is no room for mistakes or mercy.

Darius steps back from the table, feeling hollow. The coldness of the room reaches into his bones. Another secret is born in silence. Another crack in the polished image.

The waiting area near the operating rooms is basic—just a sad plant, hard chairs set neatly, and a coffee machine smelling of burnt grounds. The fluorescent lights make the tired air feel heavier. The vending machines hum without care.

Darius stands stiffly by the coffee machine. His scrubs are damp at the neck, and blood stains his sleeve a rusty color. The machine's hum hides his shaky breath. His hands, so steady minutes ago, now hang loose. His face is pale in the dull light, and his eyes look empty, like a field after a storm with nothing left.

The doors open with a soft sound. Caius Drake enters calmly but with a strong presence. He fills the room not by noise, but by his firm bearing—his shoulders strong, his voice quiet but hard. He looks at the clock—3:23 a.m.—then fixes his eyes on Darius, judging him. Caius carries the weight of many years watching men rise and fall.

He doesn't offer sympathy. He adjusts his coat and steps closer, like gravity pulling him forward.

"You know," Caius says low, "the Brotherhood's protection has rules." His words are sharp and cold. "We help those who don't fail in the light. Tonight, all eyes are watching—our eyes and theirs. You can't let your mistakes cast shadows where we stand."

Darius says nothing. His knuckles whiten as he grips a chair. He breathes in the coffee smell but feels cold inside. He knows this speech well: the Brotherhood's help can be taken away like a favor. His mind replays the blood, the flatline, his voice announcing the time of death. It plays over, painfully slow.

Caius moves closer, light casting hard lines on his face. He places his hand on the table, fingers spread as if marking territory. "If this leaks, if others smell blood in our house?" He glances sharply at the vending machine, as if even its noise is a threat. "There won't be time for regret.

We bury our own mistakes—or they bury us." His voice hardens, like iron beneath velvet. "No one is irreplaceable. Not you. Not me."

"You came to control the damage, then," Darius says finally, his voice rough and quiet. "Or is this a warning? I know what's at stake. I won't show weakness."

Caius doesn't look away. "You'll do more than hide it. No weakness—not for a Hale. Fix your face, fix your story, and make sure every nurse, every board member, every tech here remembers why you were chosen for the Brotherhood." He pauses, as if about to soften, but doesn't.

Darius feels tightness in his throat but keeps quiet. The urge to defend or break is strong inside him. Instead, he swallows it down. Silence is safer. His thoughts race: the failed surgery, the looks in the hall, the cold comfort of the Brotherhood's shield. They only protect those without stains. He both needs them and hates needing them.

"You've done worse," Caius says softly, almost a whisper. "But the world has never seen." He straightens with slow purpose, casting a long shadow on the floor. "We'll control the story for now. But if you make this a habit—if you forget the rules—don't expect a next warning." He leans in close, his breath sharp with mint and coffee. "You are not alone unless you choose to be."

Darius feels both threat and help in those words. He understands: mercy here is a duty, not kindness.

Caius lets the silence grow.

"Rest," he says finally, firm. "You need your mind. You need your mask."

The order hangs in the air. With one last sharp look, Caius turns and walks away, his steps steady, his coat edges catching the harsh fluorescent light. The door closes quietly, muffling the world.

Darius stands alone, surrounded by vending machine hums and distant ventilation. The bitter taste of old coffee stays on his tongue, mixed with shame. He stays upright by the cheap chair, afraid to sit—afraid to drop the mask before he's truly alone.

Nurses gather by the break room coffee machine, their voices low and shaky under the flickering lights. The clinking of ceramic cups hides their whispers; steam rises, smelling of burnt coffee. Marisol pours, her hands shaking, glancing at her friend and then toward the door. Her worry shows in her bitten lip and quick eyes.

"Did you see? He hesitated. I swear he checked the chart twice," says a younger nurse, her words spilling out fast, as if wanting to make sure no one overhears.

Marisol whispers back, "He never hesitates. Not Darius Hale. But..." She stops as the door opens and a surgical resident comes in, his white coat neat over scrubs. Marisol straightens with a polite smile. The chat dies suddenly.

The resident doesn't nod or smile. He keeps his head down, stiff, as if he's protecting himself. He pretends not to hear the silence, but the nervous shuffle of paper cups shows tension.

Nearby, outside radiology, voices echo softly. The smell of antiseptic is strong. A respiratory therapist lowers her mask to breathe. Her hair is tied back roughly. She tells a technician quietly, her hands shaking slightly.

"Did you hear? It was Hale. He lost the middle-aged patient from Three-East. No one thought he would die."

The tech shrugs while looking at his tablet, the blue light on his face. "Doesn't matter who you are. There are stories of 'miracle men' before. But there are also cover-ups." He looks up at a security camera, half-smiling as if daring fate to prove him wrong.

The therapist bites her cheek, doubt heavy in her mouth. "If the board covers this, the word will get out. Someone is already talking to administration."

Further down, in the doctors' lounge, three doctors talk nervously by the window. City lights blur outside. The oldest, Dr. Lin, leans forward, her arms on her knees.

"They'll blame the equipment. Or say it was a fluke," she says quietly. "But it was Hale's case. You can feel the vultures."

"Do you think admin will protect him?" asks a younger doctor, fidgeting.

"He's Brotherhood gold. I heard Victoria Grant is writing a statement."

"Or finding a scapegoat," Lin says. She leaves the thought hanging.

Their silence is heavy, full of memories of previous fallen surgeons, quick press releases, and urgent early meetings.

At the nurses' station, pale light shines over polished surfaces. Darius walks in carefully, his footsteps clear but controlled. Nurses at monitors tense up as he passes. Machines beep quietly. They seem to pull away, eyes down, avoiding him.

One nurse, Amanda, looks at him briefly, nodding with quiet sympathy. His eyes pass over her, unreadable and guarded. Voices lower as he walks by; some look at papers, others at empty cups. No one reaches out.

The air feels cold on his skin. He tastes metal, panic, and failure in every breath. The pressure on his chest tightens—an invisible grip.

Whispers cling to the edges of his memory, shaping into unspoken judgments that tighten his spine. People say he missed something. Lost his skill. Or worse—broke under pressure, the golden talent revealed as flawed. The shadows of the Brotherhood seem longer down these hallways, darker than the light.

In this hospital, a place built on order, reputation, and secrets, every mistake is a weapon for those in power. Rumors become attacks from rivals. Darius knows deep down that opponents will use this moment to spread gossip. The hospital's social order balances on a sharp edge, sharpened by ambition and secret deals. The Brotherhood's power moves through every exchange, unseen but felt. A mistake is never just a mistake. It opens cracks in control, and watchful eyes track every break.

He keeps walking. The corridor feels longer with each step. His shadow stretches thin and narrow. Heads bow farther as he passes, the tapping of keys and scattered papers filling the space he leaves behind. With every step, he feels farther from the world—each silent face another thread in the growing web of suspicion.

His back prickles as he passes the nurses' station; the sting of being an outsider is sharper than the antiseptic burn on his skin. In this sudden quiet, judgment waits—not only in curious eyes but as a force shaping halls and futures.

He walks steadily down the hall, his steps breaking the whispers, silencing rumors, even as the watchful eyes stay close.

Darius pushes open his office door, the soft thud feeling loud in the quiet after midnight. The blue glow of the corridor lights shines through the door crack, barely lighting the dark room inside. He leans against the cool door, his breath shaky and thin. The hospital's silence fills the space, swallowing the last sounds from the OR: the flatline beep, muffled gasps behind masks, and the steady passing of instruments.

He finally moves, crossing to his desk with the weight of invisible chains on his shoulders. His fingers touch the smooth desk edge—almost comforting. The air smells faintly of disinfectant and latex, reminders of sterile work. He sits in the chair. Surgical tools are laid out carefully next to a thick folder with the dead patient's chart. A scalpel shines under the desk lamp, casting sharp reflections. Darius closes his hand around the scalpel handle, finding ritual in the touch.

For a brief moment, the outside world fades. He is back in the hard world of the OR. The scene plays in his mind: his calm voice calling for the clamp, the resident's nervous glove, precious seconds lost, the patient's chest moving weakly under bright lights. He feels the patient's pulse stop under his hand—nothing left.

Not just tonight. His memories break into pieces—the feeling of earlier victories flashes sharply. Saving a woman who collapsed after a car wreck, fixing the heart of a senator's daughter with steady hands, the rush of relief and pride as monitors return to normal and the team looks at him in awe. He built a reputation in those moments: the surgeon who never panics, the hero of the OR. Each success was another stone in the myth of Dr. Hale, unbreakable.

But now the failures crowd close. Tonight's was different. He remembers clearly when it all changed: the unstoppable bleeding, the clamp not holding, the flatline relentless. Guilt bites inside him, sharper than any tiredness. He squeezes the scalpel so hard it almost breaks his gloved skin, seeking pain that can drown shame.

He breathes shakily and sets the scalpel down, almost carefully, as if it could testify against him. The manila folder nearby shows the patient's name in black ink: another person he couldn't save. The Brotherhood's plaque stares back at him—a golden emblem of a star crossed by a serpent—glowing in the lamp light like it's watching him and judging. Years chasing this symbol, giving up himself to meet its demands behind hospital walls and glass towers. The Brotherhood offers power and protection, but only if you are perfect—no mistakes, no weaknesses, or everything falls apart.

He lies to himself, but he can't stop the thoughts looping in his head: Did I miss a sign? Was my decision wrong—too sure, too slow? Will the board cover this as Brotherhood business or toss me aside for appearances?

He hears an old voice in his mind: "You can't show weakness here. Ever." Caius's words feel like iron under his skin.

The room feels smaller. He stares at the emblem, his jaw tight, his hands shaking on the desk. Everything—the myths, hidden deals, unspoken promises—demands silence. The dead man's face floats behind closed eyes. Not a number, but a life lost under harsh lights. The hospital's failures rarely reach the city's bright skyline, but here, in his office and mind, they pile up like poison dust.

He wants to scream, but he keeps quiet. Holds in his sorrow. He cannot afford to break. To break is to let the wolves—scandals, rivals, enemies—close in.

He presses his knuckles to the desk, feeling his muscles strain. Cold spreads through his arms and chest, settling deep.

He breathes in, tasting metal and stale air. He promises not to let this pain escape. The Brotherhood's strength comes from hiding the cracks, from never showing weakness—so he shuts down, locks his pain inside with cold routine. The city glows gold and bruised purple outside the small window, as if the sky is unsure how grief looks.

He forces his body to stay still, wrapping calm around him like a shield. Hours pass. Outside, the first light threatens a storm, but inside his office, silence grows heavier.

He doesn't move. Failure settles deep and silent as night turns slowly toward a cold, unsure morning.

Nurse on the Night Shift

Blood pools under the stretcher just as it stops in Trauma Bay 4. The bright hospital lights cast shadows on Lila Moreno's arms as she puts on her purple gloves, the snapping sound breaking the quiet night. The smell of blood and old cleaning chemicals fills the air. Paramedics shout information—male, sixteen years old, gunshot wound to the stomach, heart beating fast but weak. The boy's chest rises and falls shallowly. His hospital gown is stained and stuck to the stretcher. He's sweating lightly at his hairline; his lips are pale, almost blue.

"Start an IV line. Get Dr. Liang and Roy here now. Crash cart, quickly!" Lila speaks clearly and firmly as she checks the boy's wrist for a vein. His heartbeat under her thumb is weak. The room becomes busy with quick movements. IV tubes snake over the boy's arms. Monitors show green and yellow lights, reflecting in his eyes wide with fear.

Outside the glass door, a woman's loud crying cuts through the hospital noise—deep and raw. Lila briefly looks up and sees the boy's mother collapsed by the door, her hands tangled in black hair, tears on her face. The technician tries to pull a curtain, but Lila moves past machines and kneels on the cold floor. She takes the mother's cold hands in hers.

"He's fighting," Lila says, pressing until they feel their pulses match. "I promise I won't stop until he's safe. We won't lose him tonight." The mother's eyes lift to Lila's, searching and glassy. Lila holds the look, calming the grief for a moment with the comfort of touch. It's not empty—her hands steady the mother, reminding her of her own brother's fragile hope.

Lila rises quickly, moving past curtains and blood-stained shoes, back to the boy's side before the monitors can alarm. A new medic's hands shake as he opens a vial, his eyes flicking to instructions taped near the crash cart. He reads the label wrong and draws too much medicine. Lila notices the mistake—the bead of sweat on his lip, the nervous look, the pause as he pulls the drug. She stops his syringe in mid-air.

"That's twice the dose he needs," she says quietly but firmly. "Check the chart—half the dose for his weight and age." The medic's face turns red. He nods and tries again. Lila doesn't blame him—she just corrects calmly, adjusting the dose without fuss. She signals Roy to check vital signs, her steady presence organizing the chaos around her.

"All clear? Next, monitor and suction, then ultrasound," she says, and the emergency room works smoothly again. She is both a strong leader and gentle support. In moments like this, she sees their shared struggle—the medic's fear, Roy's focus, Dr. Liang's concern with the ticking time. Lila brings them together. She remembers Dr. Hale's cold approach on hard nights: smart but distant. She chooses warmth, mixing urgency and care, fighting for the boy and for the team to keep hope alive.

Emma Hayes moves quickly, pushing a stretcher with skill. She stops by the curtain and nods to a new machine glowing blue and silver. "See? They got us a portable ultrasound. Guess the board wants to show off for donors." Her voice is light, but her eyes watch the machines closely. Equipment like this is rare here, as the department is always short of supplies. Emma's joke holds a truth: new gear often comes with strings attached, more control, not just help.

"Maybe next week we'll get that coffee machine you've been asking for," Lila replies, a small smile hidden in her tight lips.

"From their lips to God's ears," Emma says as she moves on to use the new device.

Alarms go on and off around them; the ventilator's noisy breath fills the room. Lila wipes sweat from her forehead, burning salt in her eyes. Chaos comes in waves—voices, footsteps, electronic sounds measuring life by numbers. Her nerves are tight, but her hands don't shake. She breathes in cold, clean air and looks up as the trauma alarm sounds again, another emergency rushing in. She straightens up and jumps back into the flow, her heart focused on hope as shouts and quick steps grow louder, showing no rest will come before morning.

The staff break room glows with dull overhead lights and the low sound of vending machines giving out the same stale snacks each night. Lila's shoes squeak on the linoleum floor as she enters, a dried blood stain spreading on her navy scrubs. The bitter smell of coffee mixes with the sharp scent of sanitizer on her skin.

At one end, two people sit turned away from the door, whispering. Victoria Grant, dressed in a sharp suit, taps her nail on her tablet while talking to a heavy board member. Lila hears bits of their talk: "...good credentials, but not surprising with donors backing. Trauma director jobs aren't given just on skill anymore."

Lila stops by a worn couch, twisting a paper towel nervously as she watches. She sees Victoria's cold smile and the board member's quiet laugh. "Generous donors," Victoria says with emphasis, "expect something in return."

The room feels smaller. Nurses gather in small groups, dropping their voices as Emma Hayes comes in with two chipped mugs. She pours coffee and slides one to Lila, steam rising between them.

"These donors don't just give money," Emma says quietly, nodding toward Victoria. "They pretty much run this place now. No one says no to their wishes—not unless they want trouble." She smiles but looks tired and worried.

"It's getting out of hand," Lila says, looking at the door. "You can't even change how we treat patients without asking the donors first." She keeps her shoulders tight. "When did helping patients become something you have to ask permission for?"

A nurse sips from a thermos, watching the board members carefully. Others—orderlies, interns—quiet down, making themselves smaller. Through the window in the door, Lila sees a supervisor walk by; silence follows him.

Emma leans close, lowering her voice. "Half the nurses are scared to complain about staffing. Victoria has eyes everywhere. Remember last week when Roy asked for more supplies?" Emma makes a mocking gasp, then gets serious. "Three hours later, supply emails about 'cost control.'"

Lila holds her mug tightly, her knuckles white. "I just want to do my job," she says quietly, anger building inside. "One day we'll lose someone because the right donor didn't approve quick blood tests, and when that happens…" She stops, swallowing hard.

Emma doesn't answer right away. She taps the mug rim—one-two-three breaths steady as a heartbeat. She looks at Lila, silently asking if she'll speak up when it's needed. Is she ready to risk it?

The tension breaks when Mr. Petrov bursts in, his suit sharp and his smile forced. "Everyone," he says loudly, as if on a stage, "let's work hard for our donors tonight. The department's funding depends on their support. Let's show them thanks—their trust keeps St. Gabriel's running."

Lila's jaw tightens. Heads nod. No one argues. Petrov smiles fake and leaves.

Victoria closes her tablet with a snap and leaves with the board member. Their voices fade: "…VIP wing ready by spring. Our partners will be pleased."

Emma sighs, pushing her mug away. "It's like money decides the rules here now, not medicine." She glances at the clock—twenty minutes before the next emergency.

"They don't see what happens at three in the morning," Lila says. "Patients bleeding, doctors running on exhaustion, pharmacy locked behind passwords some executive set up." Her hand shakes as she sets down the empty mug, moving carefully despite her growing anger.

"I'm not going to stand by while they decide what matters," she says loudly. Emma meets her eyes, a faint smile of support and hope.

Lila leaves the mug in the sink, a small drop of coffee on her finger before she wipes it. The room's light flickers cold and blue-white. She stands tall and pulls the door open, jaw tight, carrying bitter resolve in her throat. Behind her, the break room hums with quiet fear and the clear truth that this place is no longer fully theirs.

Lila checks her watch: 4:17 a.m. Her eyelids feel heavy after a double-length shift, tiredness in her bones like the buzz of the hospital lights. Outside, it's still dark, morning just an idea, not a promise. She leans against the wall, rubbing her temple, then slips quietly into the medication room. Cool air, sharp with cleaning smells, sticks to the sweat under her scrubs. On metal shelves, trays of IV bags and labeled vials wait. Farther away, hospital sounds drift—alarms, quiet voices, wheels on floors. She breathes in, pictures home, her brother asleep behind a locked door. That thought fades; that world feels far from her own need here. She steadies herself, fingers moving fast on the digital pad, updating the heart patient's complex medication schedule—a code she must not mess up.

She leaves the room with a quick step and sits on a cracked plastic chair at the nurses' station. The desk is a mess: crumpled papers, scattered pencils, cold cups with forgotten tea. The smell of sanitizer mixes with tired bodies. Lila opens a chart, blinking away grit as she checks labs, meds, and allergies blurring together. Her hand shakes as she reaches for a bottle of digoxin, almost reading the wrong label. She shakes her head, warning herself, and counts tablets carefully. Nearby, a younger nurse fumbles with a dose, writing down the wrong decimal. Lila sees the mistake and moves over, her voice soft and kind:

"That dose will slow his heart dangerously. It's too high."

The young nurse's eyes grow wide, worry showing.

"It's okay," Lila says with a tired smile. "Let's check it again together."

A quiet moment passes as Lila fixes the chart and slides the right dose forward. The nurse breathes out a shaky thanks. Lila goes back to her work, exhaustion tugging at her eyes, the memory of many tough nights pulling at her patience, teaching hard-earned kindness from endless work and no mistakes allowed.

Among alarms and the hiss of a coffee machine, she finds a moment of calm. Lights above flicker, casting blue and brown shadows in the hall. She pulls out her phone, feeling her pulse more than her footsteps. She reads a message from Mateo: Safe. Home. Did you eat? She types back fast: Door locked; you better be asleep. Love you. Her thumb hesitates; she wishes she could give her brother the kind of safety she offers strangers. Worry tugs like a ghost hand, reminding her that outside the hospital, the world can turn bad suddenly. She puts the phone away and straightens her shoulders.

Emma appears around the corner, laughing softly. She pulls gum from her pocket with a raised eyebrow.

"Still standing? I swear you run on this stuff. I'm half sure there are actual caffeine IVs in those cabinets."

Lila manages a half smile, half grimace. "Chewing gum's cheaper than a second heart transplant. Barely."

Emma leans back, laughing. "That's why you get the superhero badge tonight. Sit down for five minutes. I'll tell Petrov you're meditating in the supply room—mandatory enlightenment after midnight." She presses the gum into Lila's hand, her voice soft but firm with the deep friendship built during countless emergencies. "Really. If you mess up another dose, I'll drag you to the break room myself."

Lila smiles, grateful behind the joking face. "Deal. Unless aliens invade before sunrise."

They share a look, tied together by years of overtime—a silent promise to watch out for each other, sometimes the only thing keeping them going in a job that never ends.

Lila fixes her badge, tucks her hair back, and nods at Emma, her thanks deeper than words. The hallway shines with soft light, the air sharp with the promise of morning and chaos. Alarms ring down the hall—a new ambulance, a rush of voices and feet. Lila joins the moving crowd, spearmint fresh on her tongue, her heart ready for whatever the dawn brings.

First Collision

Shift change at St. Gabriel's is a busy time—people moving from one ward to another, doctors and nurses rushing by machines that beep regularly. The bright lights leave no place for secrets, but behind calm faces and quick hellos, secrets still exist. Two surgical residents lean close at the nurse's station, their tired voices low and wary.

"Third time this week he's missed debrief," one says, looking at the on-call board where Darius Hale's name glows.

The other barely replies, "He hasn't looked at us since Ellis." The name of a patient who died still hangs heavy in the air. Everyone knows Darius Hale is troubled but untouchable.

Nearby, nurses gather over clipboards and coffee. A senior nurse, her gray hair pulled tight, lowers her voice. "You saw how the board dealt with Hale's case, right? Or maybe you didn't." She nods toward the hall, her voice bitter. "When you have the Brotherhood's money backing you, rules slip. I've seen his surgery times moved to fit his schedule, consultants canceled like that. No one else gets away with snapping orders or punishing whole shifts that cross him."

A young nurse fidgets with her badge. "He never gets in trouble. Sometimes I wonder if he could walk through a wall if he wanted."

The older nurse smiles grimly. "Try standing up to him. You'll be on night shifts fast."

Some weak laughter follows as someone approaches.

Lila Moreno leans against the medicine cart, arms crossed tight. She listens, her jaw tight, eyes unreadable, watching power control the room. The Brotherhood is like a shadow here—rumors of secret deals and money that buys silence faster than medicine dulls pain. On the staff, people change their words and lower their voices, showing the Brotherhood's real presence.

She tries to focus on small sounds—the squeak of shoes, sweat on her arm—but she feels angry. It's not just about Darius Hale. It's about the unspoken rules—how only people with the right family name avoid punishment, and respect is forced by fear. Even now, quiet voices warn: say too much, question him, and the whole system crushes you.

A careless comment breaks the quiet: "Nobody dares cross him. Even attendings avoid him." Lila's voice cuts in sharply. "Enough. We all have work. Gossip doesn't help unless it changes how we care for patients." Her words hit like a challenge in a room where challenges often die.

Some glance at her—grateful, cautious. The silence she creates is different—not fear, but something strong and clear. Her anger heats her throat.

The quiet spreads down the hall like spilled ink. People freeze as footsteps come—cold and steady—the man everyone notices more when he's gone than when he's there.

Darius Hale walks down the hall as if through fog. His passing chills the air; monitors beep softly, conversations stop, and colleagues press close to walls with their eyes down. He doesn't look at anyone—not the whispering residents, nurses, or Lila. His white coat is clean except for a faint dark mark under his eye—a small crack in his armor, visible only to those who know where to look.

He moves on, each step cutting through the room's tension. The staff parts, not out of respect but to avoid his power. No one breathes until the double doors close behind him, his exit barely making a sound.

"Turned a cold wind in here, didn't he?"

"Wouldn't want to be anyone but him—" a tech begins but stops under Lila's stare.

Lila straightens, her body tense, silently refusing to back down. She watches Darius leave, the quiet left behind swallowing sound. She makes a promise—not just as a nurse, but as a sister, fighter, and woman who knows what oppression feels like. She won't shrink from the cold or the unspoken rules that let men like him go unchecked.

Not today. Not ever.

She moves forward, a quiet defiance running through St. Gabriel's.

In the staff room, a flickering light casts weak illumination over tired walls and lockers. The break table has half-empty mugs, sticky notes, and a patient sheet curling in the heat of the afternoon shift change. Nurses and junior doctors drift in between rounds. Lila Moreno stands by the whiteboard, holding a worn patient file.

She looks at her reflection on the marker-streaked board—dark eyes clear, jaw set, knuckles tight around the folder. The smell of antiseptic lingers on her fingers, her badge shining in the light. The group near the coffee maker quiets as she speaks, cutting through the slow gossip poisoning the air outside.

"I think if we spread out the doses, we'll avoid problems later," Lila says calmly. "The last tests show his potassium dropped more with each fast dose—he's sensitive. If we slow it down and balance it with fluids—" She draws a line on the board, "—we keep levels steady and avoid heart problems."

A junior doctor, new and tired, leans in, curious. Beside him, a nurse chews her pen cap, watching Lila and the chart carefully.

The door creaks open behind Lila. The mood sharpens. Darius Hale enters, his white coat perfect, holding another chart. His presence brings silence that tightens in throats.

He looks at the team, then the board. "There's a reason for protocol," he says coldly. "We don't change medication schedules alone. If you have concerns, talk after rounds, not in front of everyone." He stares at Lila. "Following the rules isn't up for debate."

Even the clock seems to stop. Someone coughs awkwardly. Lila turns fully, her arms loose but her posture strong, not folding against his stare. The hospital's hidden power plays crackle between them, shown in their body language and glances toward the door.

"With respect," Lila says, steady but firm, "people aren't diagrams. We see reactions before numbers show. Often, noticing early is why our patients leave alive." She looks at the group, then back at Darius. "Working together isn't a threat. I'm not against you—I'm doing my job, like everyone else here."

Near the window, a nurse adjusts her mask, as if hiding. A junior doctor coughs and shifts. Tension hangs in the air. Lila's heart pounds under her scrubs, steady but loud.

Darius's jaw tightens. "Following rules saves lives. This hospital runs on standards, not ideas. If you want to question me, do it somewhere else. On my shift, you follow orders. If you can't, ask for reassignment." He speaks calmly, but the words hit hard.

A fan rattles in the corner. Lila straightens, unclenching her hands, holding his gaze. She feels her own strength—it's not just about stubborn patients or rules. It's about the care her mother wanted, the kind she promised Mateo. Her values are not optional; they come from hard work and exhaustion. The cost of silence is too high.

She keeps looking at him, steady as a mountain shadow at dusk. Around her, the staff holds their breath—not friends or enemies, just watching as the hospital's order cracks.

"I'll be here all night," Lila says softly but firmly. "For my patient."

The air feels charged, tasting of old coffee and electricity—like a storm coming. Darius's face stays cold, but a flicker appears in his eyes. He turns, his coat sweeping as he leaves, tension following.

No one speaks. The quiet lasts, filled with unease, as Lila holds the file—her heart racing, but her will alive. When the usual hospital chatter starts again, everyone in that small, dim room knows St. Gabriel's is different now.

Darius's office closes behind him with a sharp click, cutting him off from the world. He stands still, his back straight, fists clenched so tightly his knuckles turn white. Rain taps against the window, city lights blurred in the dusk. The soft hum of ventilation barely blocks the ringing in his ears—the echo of his name whispered in hallways, the memory of Lila's firm voice standing up to him.

He counts his breaths, each rough and heavy. The taste of adrenaline is sharp like metal. He still sees her strong jaw and steady eyes refusing to back down. That small staff room moment made authority feel fragile, like fine china about to break.

She didn't step back like others. Years of privilege and silence gave him walls to hide behind—but she stood her ground without blinking. It annoys and excites him. It touches a wound he has kept closed since the tragedy months ago. When threatened, anger rises fast and cold. But this anger can't cover the new shame. Lila didn't just challenge his orders; she showed him the system itself might be broken.

He wants to believe his control is armor—that the Brotherhood's trust and the hospital's need protect him. His steady hands in the operating room tremble here. He wonders if the Brotherhood notices the crack. If Lucien, slow and careful, marks this day against him. Darius bites his lip, looking at his own dark reflection. He waits for answers he's afraid to ask.

Elsewhere, behind shelves of medicine and quiet machines, Lila slips into the supply room to find Emma Hayes. The air smells of antiseptic and faint coffee. Lila leans close, her voice low.

"Was I wrong to say it in front of everyone, Em?" Her grip on the file is tight, but she stands tall.

Emma shakes her head. "Someone had to call him out. People pretend the rules apply to all, but they bend when he walks by." Emma looks at the door, making sure no one hears. "Most would have stayed quiet."

"Yeah, but standing up while others look away feels lonely." Lila gives a bitter small smile. "But I won't let him silence me."

The quiet after is tense. Emma squeezes Lila's arm gently. "You're not alone. Just the first."

Down the hall, the nurses' break room hums with fresh talk. Flickering lights hang over sticky tables. Two orderlies lean over steaming cups. A tech sits on the windowsill. Their voices hum under machine beeps.

"Did you see Moreno challenge Dr. Hale? Almost stopped my heart," one orderly says, eyes wide behind glasses.

The tech smiles, opening a protein bar. "He looked rattled—never seen that before."

"Is this the start of something, or just a blip? If the Brotherhood boy loses face... who knows what happens next?" says the other, eyes on the security camera.

Their talk fades as footsteps approach, tension growing like thick soup. The feeling stays: things are shifting, small quakes threatening to break.

In the hallway linking patient wings and the main area, bright lights cast long shadows. Lila steps out, chart pressed to her chest. Her walk is slow and steady—a small act of rebellion against the rushed pace. She turns the corner and sees Darius a few steps ahead, his face closed off, eyes distant, shoulders set like he's bracing for a hit.

They meet in the middle. The space between them crackles with tension felt on the skin. Neither looks away. Lila's eyes are dark and steady, hiding challenge behind professional calm. Darius's eyes are cold at first, then something unreadable flickers in the light. Behind the silence, her heart beats strong—refusing to give in. Behind his guarded look, a fight rages: the need to control, shame's shadow, and a dangerous curiosity between them.

A patient's bell rings from a nearby room—sharp and clear. Lila turns swiftly. Darius lingers a moment, his jaw tight, then moves into the busy hall, keeping his guard up with every step.

Lila stops at the nurses' station, watching where he disappeared. Her lips press together—not in defeat but in understanding. She feels the tremor running through the hospital, the invisible lines drawn today, and straightens her back as if to say: this fight is just starting.

Cracks in Perfection

A desk lamp glows softly over Darius's office, casting quiet shadows around the room. Outside, the night blurs the city lights into streaks of color through the window. Files are scattered near him, their labels clear and sharp, but he has ignored them all day.

He sits hunched over the cool glass desk, his forearms pressing down hard. The room is so quiet that the ticking of his watch seems loud, marking each moment of what feels like failure. With his hands resting on his forehead, he closes his eyes.

His mind drifts to a memory: the Brotherhood's dining room, warm with golden light from a chandelier. The walls are dark wood, and a long table shines in the center. At the head sits Lucien Blackwell, dressed sharply, his hair streaked with silver. When he raises his glass, everyone grows quiet.

"To Darius Hale," Lucien says, his voice steady and proud. "The Brotherhood's expert—the one who never makes a mistake."

Others at the table nod and smile softly. Caius Drake's approval feels heavy with history. Darius feels the invisible weight of this honor.

He remembers the taste of the rich wine and how those words felt more like a demand than praise. Being perfect is not optional—it's as essential as breathing.

Soft sounds of forks on fine plates mix with talk of amazing medical successes. The men at the table watch one another with quiet pride, expecting faultlessness. To Darius, it feels less like a gift and more like a heavy burden.

Suddenly, his thoughts break. The sharp sound of a surgical clamp falling echoes in his mind. The steady beep of a heart monitor stops. He's back in the operating room, where the air smells of cleaning fluid and fear. Bright lights shine down, showing every small trembling movement he makes. The patient's heartbeat fades away. Silence replaces hope.

He rubs a scar under his eye, hoping to erase the pain with a simple touch. Guilt fills him deeply, like something growing inside. Lucien's praise now feels like pressure squeezing his throat. He wonders what the Brotherhood would think if they saw him now—not the strong man at his desk, but a frightened boy crushed by impossible demands.

He stays still for a long time. Outside, the wind taps against the window like a secret code he refuses to understand.

Perfection is the main thread running through his life. He recalls his early years learning from Caius, the Brotherhood's oldest member, where discipline was rigorous. Back then, success tasted sharp and exciting. Now, it's bitter and hard to swallow.

Sometimes, he dreams of being at that table again, hearing Lucien's voice praising another success. But in his dream, the glass slips from his hand, spilling red wine on the marble. The room spins with silent judgment.

These high standards have become his own harsh voice, dragging him down with whispers of consequences worse than failure: being exposed. The Brotherhood never forgives mistakes. He learned this long ago.

His jaw tightens. The tired lines on his face come not from age, but from carrying the weight of others' expectations. He's built walls around his pain so thick that even in his empty office, he feels trapped. Being alone feels safer. Even now, he imagines the Brotherhood watching him, waiting for him to fail.

A quiet knock breaks the silence—a nurse asking briefly, then falling silent after his cold answer. Outside the door, bright hospital lights and distant sounds float by, but here, inside, only the hum of machines and the soft smell of rain remain.

He stands slowly, joints stiff. For a moment, he feels dizzy, then moves to the window, pressing his forehead to the cold glass. City lights blur and flicker as if they hold the key to his peace.

A sweaty handprint marks the glass. Despite all his power—his skill, his influence, the lives he's saved—it's not enough to quiet the voice inside him that demands perfection. Tonight, that pressure is heavier than ever.

He won't cry. Instead, Darius watches the city move, clenching his teeth and holding himself stiff, trying to keep himself from falling apart.

The air at St. Gabriel's hospital smells sharp—cleaning fluid, sweat, and cold, bright lights that never soften. Nurses in blue scrubs move quickly, carrying medicine and papers, speaking loudly to be heard over the constant noise of machines. Lila Moreno stands in the middle of it all, her hands covered in ink as she sorts urgent papers.

She feels a headache starting behind her right temple, a mix of tiredness and stress. The clock reads just after two. The harsh light makes her cheekbones stand out and shadows her tired eyes. She touches a file—Mr. Holman, age twenty-eight, collapsed suddenly—when the busy noise suddenly quiets.

Darius Hale walks in sharply. His white coat is clean, his steps quick and firm, his posture stiff. For a moment, conversations stop around him; his presence commands attention—strong and serious. He holds a bundle of x-rays under his arm, the plastic crackling lightly. Most people see a legend: Hale, the surgeon who never makes mistakes.

But Lila notices his left hand trembles slightly, a small loss of control that few would catch. He grips the films tightly, his fingers pale. She thinks of stories told during late shifts: Dr. Hale never gets tired, never fails. Some say he's like marble, others that he's colder than the steel in the OR. Now, those stories seem like childish myths compared to the tired mask on his face.

He stops at the counter and looks over a CT scan on a tablet. His face is calm, a mask of control, but his mouth tightens so much it looks painful. Only his eyes reveal a hidden storm. Lila, standing nearby, sees a flash of pain kept deep inside.

She takes a small step forward, her heart beating loudly. She remembers his sharp words from yesterday, telling her to keep to her tasks, no kindness needed.

But she cares—more than she should.

Her pen hovers over a medication chart. "Dr. Hale, for bed six—Mrs. Dewhurst—should we change her blood pressure medicine tonight because of her potassium levels?" Her voice is calm and polite, professional.

He doesn't look up. His voice is sharp, but his fingers hesitate. "Keep the dose. Check her blood levels every four hours." His words are clear but rushed.

She writes the order, trying to read beyond the instructions to the stress beneath. After a beat, she notices his shoulders relax slightly.

He's falling apart inside, though he'd never admit it. Lila feels a sudden connection—a shared understanding. She knows the look: alone, fragile, fighting to hold on before falling apart.

Her phone rings, breaking the moment. It's her brother Mateo, her emergency flashing on the screen. Duty pulls her one way—family, patients, crisis—but something keeps her standing next to Darius.

"Excuse me," she says quietly, but she stays. Through the glass, she watches the man everyone praises but few see clearly. He studies the next scan, knuckles white, lips tight. The loneliness hanging off him is raw and sharp. She wonders if anyone, even the Brotherhood, has seen him without his armor.

Another nurse passes by, muttering, "He's in a bad mood today." Lila nearly laughs—how wrong they are to judge so quickly.

She answers the phone with a steady voice, watching Darius's perfect, broken figure. She rethinks all her thoughts and fears. The urge to reach out and break through his mask is strong but feels dangerous.

So she decides to wait. To watch. To listen. Until he shows her the real man—the one hiding behind the surgeon's unshakable image, the one whose hands shake tonight.

The patient file closes sharply, filling the quiet office. The sound hangs between Darius and the dark window behind him. The setting sun catches his copper-colored hair and highlights his sharp face. His hand presses the binder down as if it might jump away. A small muscle twitches in his jaw. The air smells faintly like cleaning fluids and paper, but also like long hours in scrubs and a deeper unrest.

Outside, the hallway buzzes—carts rolling, voices giving orders, machines beeping. Lila stands just outside the door, her heart beating fast. She hugs her clipboard tightly, as if it might keep her rooted.

Inside, Darius moves like a man who counts every action. Lila sees the cracks—a small shake in his wrist, his eyes fixed on the desk instead of around. The tension around him chills the room.

"Dr. Hale?" she says softly, careful. "Is there anything I can do to help?"

He doesn't look up. He presses his hand on the top file like he's trying to stop a wound from bleeding. His stiff posture is like armor. When he speaks, his words are sharp and brief.

"Everything's under control, Nurse Moreno."

The way he says her name feels cold. Lila nods, fighting the wish to push past his walls. She forces a small, polite smile—the kind she uses for scared family members and difficult patients—but it feels weak and false.

She steps out and closes the door quietly behind her. The hallway's bright lights feel harsh, making the world seem raw. She hears laughter, a code blue paging over the intercom, machines humming, but none of it calms her.

For a moment, she stays, her hand on the doorframe, her thumb tracing the worn wood. She wants to believe all these locked doors and secrets could be opened with the right words. She wants to believe she isn't on the edge of being pulled under.

She looks back without meaning to. Darius hasn't moved. He is a dark shape framed by light: face half-hidden, jaw clenched, a statue hiding a quiet storm.

Memories push in: the first time she saw him in the operating room—his hands moving with skill and cold focus. It wasn't just talent; it was shutting down all feeling to work perfectly. But what haunts her is what comes after—the empty look in his eyes, the way he shuts down after surgery, as if guilt punishes and protects him at once. The stories of him as unbreakable fall apart when she sees that small tremble now.

Her mind races: stay safe or step in? Pull back or reach out? She knows enough secrets—her own and others'—to see the warning signs behind his calm. The Brotherhood's presence looms over the hospital, silent and heavy, and approaching it is risky.

Caring is dangerous, she tells herself. It can burn you, draw you in, make you responsible. She can't fall apart—not for him or anyone else—but the urge to help burns inside her.

She remembers their recent fight, his cold words. Still, now, the loneliness she sees in him is deeper than any punishment she could give. Part of her wants to stay.

Inside, Darius sits very still, shoulders tight, as if holding all the day's weight. The silence between them is full of unspoken words neither dares to say.

Lila lets out a shaky breath and drops her hand from the doorframe. For a moment, she wants to run, to protect herself. But her eyes rest on the crack under the door where light falls into shadow, and she wonders if it's already too late to act like she's not drawn to him.

The world continues: voices, orders, machines humming. Lila walks away, but the space behind her feels tight, pulling her back to the darkness in that office. She doesn't look back again—but the heaviness of Darius at his desk follows her down the hall—unshakable and real.

Unwanted Concern

The hallway on the third floor of St. Gabriel's is mostly empty, except for the steady hum of the lights above. The fluorescent lights flicker nervously, casting long, strange shadows on the clean linoleum floor and the dull blue walls. The cleaning crew is gone; the only sounds are Lila's sneakers tapping on the shiny floor and Darius's quick, almost robotic steps ahead of her.

He walks ahead, shoulders straight, his white coat half off, hanging from his arms as if he can't decide whether to take it off or keep wearing it. He moves with a brittle kind of energy, as if anger and tiredness are the only things holding him up.

Lila catches up, determined not to let him disappear this time. She steps right in front of him, blocking his way. Her hospital badge swings slightly as she grips it tightly, her knuckles turning white.

"Don't walk away," she says quietly but firmly, even though her voice shakes a little. "Not tonight." The words break the silence, and for a moment, they both stand still, surrounded by the hospital's clean, antiseptic smell—a smell full of broken promises and desperate hope.

Darius's eyes look past her, focused on something she can't see. She feels the tension in his body, like the electricity before a storm. His arms cross over his chest, his whole body showing that he's resisting. He gives her a cold, sideways glance.

"You should be going home, Nurse Moreno. Your shift is over."

If he had lost his temper, she might have let it go. But his cold, formal voice makes her stand firm.

"I'm not leaving until you answer me. Not as your nurse, not as someone who just falls in line." Lila takes a deep breath, finding strength she didn't know she had after so many sleepless nights. "Don't you get tired of pretending everything's fine when you're falling apart? One minute you're here, the next you shut yourself off. I see you, Darius—even when you try to disappear."

He doesn't react at first. For a moment, there's only the hum of the lights and Lila's heartbeat in her ears.

"I don't know what you mean." His words are sharp and cold; she almost flinches.

"You do," she says softly now, looking him straight in the eye. "I care, even if you don't want me to."

He tenses, his jaw working as he chooses silence. In his eyes, she sees a brief crack—a break in his tough exterior.

"This isn't about me," he says quietly. "You'd do better to focus on what you can fix. Some burdens can't be shared."

She shakes her head, refusing to back down. "I know what it's like to carry things alone. That's not strength. My brother Mateo shut me out before, but I wouldn't let him. I won't let you either."

He relaxes his fists a little, his fingers twitching. She notices and feels a small, hopeful spark—even if it's fragile.

"Why do you care?" he asks quietly, almost whispering.

"Because I've seen people I love drown in silence," she says softly. "And I won't just stand by if it's happening again—if I can do something."

He hesitates, looking past her to the dark hall beyond. When he looks at her again, the hard mask slips briefly, showing raw pain.

"I can't talk about it," he says. His shoulders drop a little. "Some things go beyond this hospital. Asking questions can cost you more than you think."

Lila's heart races. "Maybe that's a risk I'm willing to take."

He swallows hard. For a moment, she sees the real person—afraid, uncertain, close to breaking or asking for help. But then he hides it again, shutting down whatever warmth tried to break through.

"Don't," he says softly, and it hurts.

He steps back and turns away, swallowed up by the empty hallway's mix of light and shadow. Lila stands alone, her badge trembling in her hand, feeling like a door has closed—and something dangerous waits behind it.

Outside a narrow window, rain paints silver streaks on dark glass, running down to a glowing concrete area where the night maintenance workers laugh quietly. The hallway hums with the steady buzz of the lights. Darius stands still by the glass, his strong jaw reflected faintly.

Behind him, soft footsteps approach. Lila's scent—sharp with antiseptic and wet cotton—fills the air. He doesn't turn. She stops close, her shoes silent on the polished floor.

"You're walking away like you think I won't follow," she says, her voice nearly lost in the hospital noises. "But I'm here at this hour, too."

He stays silent, looking at the floor tiles. Outside, a siren wails then fades. He swallows, pained, and replies softly, "Some parts of this hospital are better faced alone."

Lila laughs quietly. "Sure. But here you are, staring out at locked doors from the only window with a view. What do you think you see?"

His gaze sharpens, briefly catching her reflection. She is steady, her hospital badge swinging nervously from her neck. Darius wants to warn her, but she is close enough to feel her warmth. His voice drops to a quiet whisper.

"People think this place is simple—lights above, orderlies below, break room rules. They see schedules, meetings, rumors. But they don't see the people who run it all from behind the scenes."

"You mean the donors?" she asks, trying for a joke. "Or the ghosts?"

He shakes his head stiffly. "No. Ghosts make less noise than the real rulers. There are groups—call them circles or alliances—that expect us to do much more than our jobs. They decide who gets hired, who gets treated, and who gets research money. They know details about you that don't matter to others. They keep secrets and punish those who ask questions. You've seen the donor plaques, the empty private wings, sudden changes in leaders."

A cleaning cart rattles somewhere down the hall. The janitor looks back and keeps walking. The lights flicker, making cold shadows. Lila's shoulders tense as she looks at Darius's pale face and tired eyes.

"You think I'll run away just because things look darker here?" she says. Her hand lifts, then drops. "You act like you're the only one with something to lose, but you're not. I won't just watch you drown in silence."

Darius looks calm on the outside, but inside he feels old pain—duty choking him, guilt biting deep. For years, a group called the Brotherhood kept the hospital running: making sure the ER got resources, protecting reputations with phone calls. Sometimes this meant hiding small truths to keep control. Each plaque in the lobby, each locked door, was part of this secret control. Most staff accepted the routine—weekend shifts, new rules, endless schedules. But the true leaders worked in secret chats, private dinners, and quiet deals. Darius once believed this order kept people safe. Now it only sickens him. His isolation is both armor and punishment, helping him protect his heart while others circle like sharks just out of sight.

"You don't understand," he says, his voice breaking. "Here, asking questions costs more than comfort. There are rules, and if you break them, people disappear—moved, fired, sometimes worse."

Lila stays firm, fingers tapping her badge like a heartbeat. "What about you? Do you just follow orders and call it loyalty? Or does it hurt when you watch someone slip away?"

He flinches.

"You think you're doing the right thing, Darius, but you lock everyone out. You warn, but you don't trust. Not yourself, not me. Why not give me a reason not to be afraid?"

His eyes lift, jaw tight, hands clenched. "If you care about yourself, leave this alone. Whatever you think you see, ignore it. For your own good."

For a moment, they just breathe. Lila wants to say more—wants to pull him out of the darkness—but Darius steps back, disappearing into the shadows down the hall. His footsteps make no sound. She stands between the flickering lights and the hospital's quiet after hours. The hall seems longer, full of danger and unknowns, as her breath clouds in the cold air.

The staff lounge at St. Gabriel's is barely comfortable. Cheap fluorescent lights shine on worn couches and chipped mugs. The air smells like old coffee and disinfectant, with the low buzz of a vending machine swallowing coins. The only window is a thin slit showing city lights blurred by rain and distance.

Darius sits in a corner at a plastic table, fingers wrapped around a cold paper cup. His shoulders are hunched, and shadows deepen under his eyes. He stares ahead, still and hard, as if he's trying to disappear.

Lila enters quietly, but he notices: his fingers tense, his breathing pauses. She closes the door softly, crosses the room past untouched mugs, and pulls out a chair across from him. Her hospital badge shines slightly as she sits.

Neither speaks at first. Outside, the hospital's night shift whispers: an elevator, a supply cart rolling by, faint laughter from the ER. Inside, silence feels heavy with things left unsaid.

Lila folds her hands on the scarred table, watching Darius intently. She sounds tired but strong.

"I don't understand," she says quietly. "You push everyone away. Not just now. You act like you don't care when people worry about you or try to help. You pull back even more. Like none of it matters." She traces an old ink stain on the table. "If you keep doing this, Darius, you're going to break."

He stays still, his eyes flicking sideways like he's watching for danger. His voice is slow and flat.

"What do you want me to do, Lila? Pretend? Open up? Fall apart in the hall so everyone sees I'm not strong?"

Her lips part, nervous. "I'd just like some honesty." She leans forward. "Let someone see what really is inside, even for a moment. Isn't that what people do when they care?"

His silence makes the air heavy. He presses his palms on the cup, staring down as if ready for pain. After a long pause, he breathes out slowly.

"We can't afford that. In the Brotherhood, weakness is danger. There's no space for doubt or grief. No one shows their wounds—not even to themselves. You numb everything or you lose everything."

Those words hit hard. Beneath his tough mask, Lila senses a fragile pain.

She wants to argue, to shake him awake, but remembers her brother Mateo's silence—the way it meant pain too big to speak. She softens but keeps her worry sharp.

"You think pushing everyone away makes you strong? My family survived because we let each other in, even when it hurt and wasn't safe. You can't live behind walls and call it living. That's not strength. That's hiding."

She almost reaches for his hand, but stops. Their hands hover close, not touching, but the space between sparks.

He doesn't pull away. His dark eyes meet hers, heavy with regret and longing. There's something flickering inside him she wants to understand.

"If I let down my guard," he says, "I don't know what's left. I don't know what you'd find."

Her voice is shaky but steady. "I'm not leaving. Not until you trust me. Not until you try."

For a moment, they say nothing. The hospital sounds fade, leaving only soft breathing and the vending machine's hum. Two people stand on opposite sides of an invisible gap, neither willing to give up. Fear and hope mix—the chance of pain and the chance of healing.

He looks at her, really looks, and the world feels full of danger and possibility. Their silence is heavy with everything said and unsaid, as if the city outside is holding its breath just for them.

Rain Against Glass

Between the last quiet moments and the constant hum of machines in the hospital, the ICU lights flicker. Shadows move, and then everything—sight, control, hope—falls into deep darkness, broken only by the sudden wailing of alarms. The hallways beyond are just shapes and sounds; even the emergency red lights here at St. Gabriel's Hospital seem weak, their red glow slowly moving along the floor and metal bed rails, more warning than comfort.

For a moment, the staff move like small bursts of energy in the dark. Emma Hayes moves with steady skill, holding her radio tightly, her calm voice cutting through the tension. Two new doctors search in the dark, feeling for pulses and checking equipment by touch alone. At bed six, Lila Moreno's face is lit by her flashlight, her features sharp in the light and shadow as she leans over tubes, holding the handle as if she's keeping a breaking world together.

The smell of antiseptic mixes with rising panic—the old floor sweating, the nervous plastic of gloves, the chemicals making the place feel ancient and dangerous. Lila opens her mouth to speak but tightens her hold on the flashlight, checking the drip lines, touching cold skin and sticky tape. She looks up at Emma.

"There's no oxygen output on bed eight—get someone on the ventilator." Emma nods and presses the radio button. "ICU status, code black. Repeat, ICU code black. Need backup now!"

A sharp metallic sound. Footsteps approach. The hiss of breaths given by hand. The blackout changes everything: without monitors, every heartbeat must be judged by sound and feel alone.

The doors open. Darius Hale steps in, calm and serious—his eyes narrow in the low red light. Even in the dimness, he brings a cold focus that makes Emma and Lila stand at attention. He looks at the chaos—a world on the edge. His jaw tightens, his eyes fast, counting every lost second.

His voice is clear and direct. "Emma, triage at the headwall. You two"—he points to the new doctors—"stabilize bed seven. Lila, you're on bed four—diabetic. Her insulin pump isn't working. Manual insulin, now. Move fast. If you're unsure, ask. Every minute matters."

He doesn't yell, but his words feel sharp like the cold hospital floors. Emma gives orders through the radio, and Lila, already moving, tries to calm her nerves and grabs an insulin vial. Breaths catch. A monitor nearby emits a dying beep. Darius switches on his flashlight, checking patient charts. He's taking control, dividing the work.

The ICU, usually full of high-tech tools, now feels like a battlefield. Every mistake will be noticed—by hospital leaders, rival doctors like Crowe, and board member Victoria Grant, who waits to use any error against Darius. Here, everything—ICU's reputation, Darius's career, the hospital's control—depends on getting through this. Every breath counts.

Darius moves with Lila, working closely but without true trust. They rely on touch, voice, and short, careful commands. Lila pulls insulin and a syringe, fumbling once in the dark. Darius immediately helps, gripping her hand firmly. Their brief touch sends a small shock through Lila. He looks away first, and they keep working.

A cart falls outside, clanging loudly, sending a wave through the corridor. One new doctor starts to move toward the noise, but Darius raises his hand, calm but firm. "Stay here. ICU first. Focus."

Lila watches him for any sign of weakness. He's strong—orders sharp, decisions quick. She sees his tight jaw and stiff hands holding his stethoscope. Her respect grows alongside her curiosity.

Another silence waits to be broken. Emma quietly updates vital signs—heart rate, breathing—her voice steady. Lila and Darius gather at patient four's bedside under the red light. Outside, chaos still fills the hospital halls, where every action will be remembered, and every mistake waits to hurt someone.

Darius and Lila look at each other—no masks, just need. For the first time, without words, trust replaces old grudges. Side by side, they face the unknown, the fight between medicine and darkness.

The blackout presses down, filling the ICU with heavy darkness. Only emergency red lights and flickering flashlights prevent total blackness. Darius Hale stands at the far corner, a boy lies before him, blood staining gauze and sheets. The sharp antiseptic smell fills the air, mixed with metal and fear. Darius's gloved hand hovers over the boy's chest, between broken ribs, but the moment feels blurred—blue scrubs, a collapsed lung, his rattling breath like time breaking.

His mind echoes an old alarm sound, mixed with the current one. He sees a pale face from another time—a patient who didn't survive, whose grief still haunts Darius. He smells iodine and feels cold sweat under his mask. His hand shakes suddenly. Guilt tastes like copper on his tongue.

A hand catches the nearby bed rail—Lila Moreno, her eyes wide in the dark, holding her flashlight under her arm as she leans close. The red light softens the hard lines on her face.

"You're not alone. We've got this," she says quietly, not for the boy or the nurses, but for Darius, who is caught between wound, monitor, and memory. Her words startle him. For a moment, he stares at her, almost lost before the world snaps back.

His jaw tightens. The rules of their group—the Brotherhood—are clear: never show weakness, never falter first. Weakness unravels everything—career, Brotherhood, the fragile control he fights to keep. He thinks—if anyone sees him hesitate, vultures like Victoria Grant and Sebastian Crowe will attack. They want proof that Darius Hale is just a man, and men can fall.

But Lila's hand stays, steadying him. The ICU noise continues—alarms, a new doctor swearing as she struggles with a manual breathing bag, pounding footsteps, rustling sheets. Darius focuses on the vital signs—the fast, uneven pulse, shallow breath. He pushes doubt away and nods sharply, his face set.

"Push 20 milliliters of saline now. Hold pressure here—careful, he's bleeding inside the chest," Darius says firmly. The power generator hums, steady but weak above. Nearby, Emma patches a patient's scalp, her voice soft. Two interns hurry to follow orders.

Lila moves to the other side, kneeling to get bandages, her voice calm and clear—she asks for more gauze, bumping his shoulder. Their hands brush when passing instruments, sending a brief electric jolt before they both focus back on their work. Darius watches her as she stitches a wound, calm despite the flickering light.

He hopes her calm might support him, that he could trust someone and relax. But Brotherhood rules warn him: trust can lead to being exposed, and exposure can bring ruin. Letting down his guard doesn't just risk him—it risks Lila, too. The Brotherhood's reach is long. The warning is clear: build your walls but never let anyone in.

Still, he watches her wipe blood from her hands, her jaw tight with focus, the red light drawing shadows on her face. His orders grow colder, sharper—not cruelty, but defense. Anything else feels like giving up, and giving up means death here at St. Gabriel's.

Lila stays close after the boy is stable, as if both know these moments of quiet teamwork are fragile. Darius turns to the next patient, but her presence is there, pressing against his walls. Among alarms and heavy breaths, a truth slips out: he is not as untouchable as he wants, and tonight, someone saw the crack beneath his surface.

The ICU falls into a quiet calm, as if the darkness weighs on tired bodies and damp uniforms. The noise has died down—no more desperate cries, just the low hum of nerves and shaking hands that won't stop, no matter the light. Red lights above each bed cast a blood-like glow on the shiny floors. Lila leans against the supply cabinet, her breathing steady but shallow, feeling a strange calm between disaster and what comes next.

Not far away, Darius checks a clipboard under the weak light of his flashlight. His shadow is sharp, his eyes tired and serious, mouth tight like a knife's edge.

She watches him, then steps closer. The silence makes her steps loud, the soft sound of her voice breaking the stillness. "You know," she says quietly, hinting at a smile through her worry, "my first night in the ER, an old, grumpy patient complained so much about the cafeteria chili that I gave him a popsicle just for five minutes of peace. He yelled at me for freezing his teeth. I still think I won that night."

Darius looks up, the flashlight light passing over her cheek before he moves it away. His face is tired and watchful—more stone than man—but there's a quick sparkle in his eyes she almost misses. First, he raises an eyebrow, his mask down around his neck. His breathing stays even, as if holding emotions back.

Then his lips twitch—a small, almost invisible smile—and he breathes out, softening the dark room a little. For a moment, he just looks at her, the light shaking between them like they might both break if they look away.

"Your patients survive you, then?" he asks, dry but with a hint of humor. His voice is softer than usual.

"Most of them, except the ones who can't handle bad jokes," Lila replies, smiling with her eyes. "They need extra care."

A quiet moment passes—full of tired relief, the world held at bay by glass, broken machines, and the knowledge that when everything else fails, they have each other.

Darius holds her gaze longer than he should. His look is raw and open, a moment no rules or regrets can hide. The gentle hum of the backup generator pulses through the floor, making the tired pain in his eyes settle into something soft and fragile. Gratitude tugs at him, strange and sharp, and for that brief moment, he shows it—his broad shoulders relaxing, the hard lines at his mouth softening.

"Thank you. For... staying steady," he says quietly.

She doesn't look away. No joke now, just a warm feeling that wraps around him like a hand on his chest. Suddenly, the ICU feels smaller, safer, filled with risky hope.

The lights suddenly snap back on, a loud clang announcing their return. Bright white lights flood the ward—nurses blink, patients moan, and the usual rush returns. Screens light up, and machines beep steadily. The chaotic emergency fades into normal hospital noise.

Darius pulls back first, squinting in the bright light, his mask on again. He quickly writes dose changes on the clipboard, steady and practiced. The world feels right again, but nothing is quite like before.

Lila stays a moment longer, happy to hold onto this brief calm.

As she moves to join Emma and the others, Darius looks up. Their eyes meet. The tiredness on his face mixes with a flicker of warmth—a quiet promise, a sign they survived together in the dark.

Around them, the ICU returns to its steady pace: low voices growing confident, carts rolling through halls, the sharp smell of antiseptic mixed with burnt wires and relief. No one notices the change between Darius and Lila, invisible but real. The lines between them are different now, the air heavier, like the machines and medicine won't be enough to keep them apart after this night.

Neither will forget the night the hospital went dark and they stood side by side.

The Walls He Builds

E levator doors part without a whisper, releasing Darius into hush and gold shadow. The Orion Brotherhood's private dining room looms ahead—a chamber carved out of glass and wood atop the city, sealed from the world by thick, mirrored panels. Crystal pendants hang low, bathing the scene in a muted amber glow. The scent of aged leather and smoky cedar curls in the air. Beyond the threshold, twelve men in dark suits occupy the length of an impossibly polished mahogany table—shapes reflected in the glossy veneer, faces sharpened by candlelight. No idle chatter rides the air, just the occasional clink of crystal, as if each note seals another secret beneath the surface. Lucien Blackwell sits at the head, flanked by men twice as storied and twice as silent.

Darius steps forward—shoulders square, footfalls swallowed by lush carpet. The melancholy hush devours him, every movement punctuated by the weight of unblinking eyes. He slides into the only vacant chair. The seat's padding is deep, but coldness seeps through the velvet, needling his spine. The city winks below, alien and unreachable through floor-to-ceiling windows. In this room, every boundary is absolute.

Lucien Blackwell rises with slow, seamless precision. The flicker cast by flame finds the silver streak in his hair and the faint scar along his temple. His gaze sweeps the table, then finds Darius—two flints striking in the dark.

"Dr. Hale," Lucien begins, measured as the ticking of a surgeon's metronome, "what happened in the operating theater remains within these walls. There will be no mention of error, no hint of regret, no lingering stain. You understand." There's no warmth—only the faintest vibration of steel, a verdict uttered before trial.

No one else moves. Darius's jaw is tight, fingers pressed hard together in his lap, knuckles a pale contrast against the table's sweep. Lucien doesn't blink.

"Everything has a price," an elder murmurs from Lucien's right. "Ours is trust—ours is silence. You keep your secrets, Dr. Hale, or the world devours you whole. And us with you."

A balding attorney clears his throat, his voice thin as parchment. "There are liability issues, Dr. Hale. If word escapes, it won't simply be your reputation—this institution's, the Brotherhood's, the security of everyone here will be jeopardized. Ironclad discretion is not a suggestion."

A younger member leans forward, cufflink glinting like a blade. "You're the public face of precision, Darius. Falter for a moment, and every weakness will be turned against us all."

Nods fracture the silent surface of the table. Low voices ripple, different timbres and histories blending into one: you owe us this. Dr.

Crowne at the end drums his knuckles softly, echoing the beating of a distant, unfeeling heart.

Another elder, his voice dark and smooth, leans in. "You show weakness, Doctor, you invite wolves to dinner. We clean up our own messes."

Darius's gaze drops to the crisp white of his napkin. He can hear the thrum of blood in his ears—a rhythm at odds with the stillness. It's a room of locked doors. His own breath fogs at the roof of his mouth, caught.

Lucien's eyes flick to the city and back. "This is what's demanded. Not for me. Not for you as a man. But for Orion—so our purpose survives."

A heavy, impenetrable silence follows, thick enough to choke on.

Darius's hands remain stainless and still, but tension carves trenches up his arms. The taste in his mouth is metallic, sour. He opens his lips but finds nothing soft or human to say, nothing that wouldn't echo off these polished surfaces and fossilize into Brotherhood law. Any protest dies, fossilized and buried beneath a mountain of collective expectation.

"Everything in order, then?" Lucien asks, more statement than question.

A dozen pairs of eyes fix on Darius, hollow lights masked as men. He nods, the motion barely perceptible, a muscle judgment rather than assent. The candle wicks hiss in the glass, gold dancing over white china.

The room breathes again. Spoons lift to soup, wine is swirled, the ghosts of etiquette returning like actors to the stage. Conversation splinters into murmured anecdotes—stock markets, donor galas, the price of cufflinks imported from Florence. Not a soul mentions the patient lost on Darius's table. Not a soul mentions the real reason they gathered, as if the world can't fracture if only they are silent enough.

A junior member hitches his voice an octave higher. "I hear the board wants to renovate again. New cardiac wing, maybe?"

"Only if the right donors open their wallets," another snorts. Someone laughs. Silver forks cut into gamey venison, the scent mingling with candle smoke and restraint, all flavor drained by the forced pleasantry.

Darius doesn't speak. He watches shadows bend over linen and crystal. The cold of the room climbs up through his bones, finding its echo in the hollow throb beneath his scar.

The Brotherhood has rules older than truth. In this room, the cult of secrecy is not just habit—it's doctrine, as binding as magic, erasing sins with the white-hot polish of ritual. Here, the collective image takes precedence over any individual wound, the pain buried deep enough to rot behind glass and mahogany, untouched by the world beyond.

He came into this enclave as Orion's immaculate instrument, the hand that seldom erred. Now he feels only the heavy, inexorable slide of stone doors closing—around his grief, his guilt, and the last of his voice. The Brotherhood preserves itself, and what remains of Darius is pressed flat, a man encased within myth, warmth snuffed by ceremony.

Candlelight twitches. China gleams. He sits, silent, as isolation seeps in—distant, spectral, and absolute. No one at the table meets his eye.

The lull of glass against glass. The soft tap of polished silver on mahogany. Darius barely registers the sound, only the shape of it—a private language of power in this world above the city, sealed from the chaos below. Lucien Blackwell's voice slices with deliberate calm, but Darius tastes the bitterness underneath every word. The men encircle him, shadows thrown long by chandeliers dripping with golden light. They talk of discretion now. They warn, quietly. Each syllable slips through the perfumed air and turns sharp, drawing a line between what was celebrated and what must be hidden.

He sits, hands wound tight beneath the table, the pulse in his neck beating a restless tattoo. Their words batter him—perfect control, immaculate silence, loyalty at any cost. The fine linen smells faintly of starch and smoke, a scent he associates with old books and older lies. Once, his name inspired toasts and applause in this very room, the crystal ringing as Lucien recited his triumphs. Now the celebration has sunk to polite murmurs, then to silence, and finally to this: a chorus of caution, as clinical as any incision.

He closes his eyes. For a moment, the room vanishes—replaced by the memory of praise, days when admiration left him buoyant and unbreakable. He remembers those moments as if through a glass tarnished by breath. He sees himself, steady and certain, the Brotherhood's golden surgeon. The applause had felt endless, but it never warmed him the way he'd hoped. Tonight, he realizes it had all been as conditional as the air in his lungs.

Lucien's words circle back, seamless. More reminders. Darius aches with the effort of not flinching as another board member, his voice slick with pretense, leans in.

"If anything slips—anything—there'll be no shield, Doctor Hale. Nothing between you and the world's appetite."

Darius doesn't speak. He refuses to run his tongue over the wound. The threat coils through his chest, turning the candlelight brittle inside him.

"It isn't only your reputation at stake," says a third voice, this one from a lawyer whose hands never stop tracing a pen's cap. "If you falter, you unravel everything."

A sea of faces, most familiar, some faded. Their expressions congeal into something that almost looks like pity until he realizes it's calculation. Each pair of eyes expects his agreement, not his confession. Approval becomes a hush, a collective nod, the approval that is only allowed so long as he plays the part.

The voices dull, eroding Darius's sense of self until he feels both present and mercifully absent, hovering somewhere above his own body. His mind fractures under the weight, shame burning alongside a far colder resentment. He's struck by a vision—breaking through the fragile shell of Brotherhood approval, letting truth gleam, unshielded. He imagines how quickly these men, who once lifted him up, would vanish at the first scent of vulnerability.

They keep talking, undisturbed. The mundane creeps in as if nothing's changed—dedications, hospital grants, whispers about donors. One of them jokes under his breath about the board's next target, and the laughter is thin and sterile, curdling at the edges. Darius finds no purchase in their jokes; he can only hear the clang of the past locking itself behind him.

He can't breathe. Not really. Darius stands, pushing his chair back softly. No one stops him; their conversation plugs the gap before it forms.

He slips away like a ghost. The floor-to-ceiling windows beckon, cold and immense. Beyond the glass, the city dilates—fluorescent arteries pulsing in the dark, a network of lives racing on, oblivious. His own reflection looms there, fractured against the endless geometry of lights. He takes a breath, sharp with the thinnest tang of anxiety-laced saliva, and presses his palm to the ridged scar beneath his eye—the flesh cool, the old wound tethering him to a younger, more hopeful self.

"Not exactly the hero's welcome," Lucien says from behind, his voice almost too quiet to hear. "But you understand why it must be this way."

"Is that what you call it?" Darius asks, his words clipped. "Heroism, or a well-masked execution?"

Lucien's gaze reflects in the glass, unreadable. "You're many things, Darius. Indispensable among them. It's best you remember where family ends and obligation begins."

Darius says nothing. Lucien's footsteps recede, swallowed by the ambient hush.

He remains, shoulders taut, eyes flicking between the endless city and the candlelit echo of the Brotherhood's sanctum. Bitterness lines his mouth, but beneath it, a deeper ache takes root—betrayal laced with longing. The more they insist on silence, the more he wonders if anyone in this room sees him at all.

He thinks of walls, built thick as bedrock, each layer meant to protect and insulate. Yet the deeper he burrows into control, the heavier the frost settles in him—making warmth, real warmth, unreachable.

With his hand pressed to his face, a new image intrudes: Lila, her eyes fierce and unafraid, her laughter spilling warmth into spaces he's left cold. He can nearly touch it—the possibility of something unscripted, of falling outside the Brotherhood's shadow. He yearns for an escape hatch no one in this room dares to name.

For the first time, hope—small, fierce, reckless—edges past the walls he's built. It both terrifies and steadies him, a pulse that hints at life beyond obedience and shame.

He stands alone at the glass, the city beneath sprawling and bright and impossibly distant. The taste of secrecy sits bitter on his tongue, but for one breath, one fragile moment, Darius lets himself imagine what breaking free might feel like.

Lila's Burdens

The hospital is bright with fluorescent lights before dawn. Lila sits hunched on a vinyl chair in the empty staff lounge, her knees pulled to her chest. Her scrubs are stained with blood and coffee. A medical show plays quietly on the TV, its laugh track sounding strange against the beeps and sighs of hospital machines. Outside, rain taps against the window, blurring the city's lights.

Her phone vibrates, displaying her brother's name—a name that brings both hope and worry. She answers.

"Lila?"

His voice is weak, muffled by the noise in their old apartment.

"Mateo," she whispers, trying to sound strong. Her chest feels tight, as if she's holding everything together with small pieces.

"I got the bills for the MRI and blood tests. They cost more than I earned all summer, even with help from the government." He struggles to speak. She pictures him at the kitchen table, mail spread around him, his thumb pressing the tattoo behind his ear as if it will help.

She imagines the bills: stamped "urgent," his panic as he tries not to shake.

"Have you been taking your medicine, Teo?" she asks carefully.

There's a long pause.

"Some days. I had to make them last longer. We'll manage. I just wanted to tell you before it gets worse."

She steadies herself, though she feels sick inside. "I'll handle it. Don't skip your medicine again, okay? We'll find a way. Just rest. I love you."

"Love you too. Sorry, Lila."

The call ends. She rests her forehead on her knees. The smell of cleaning chemicals mixes with old coffee and sweat. Her heart pounds. The world shrinks to the ticking clock.

She can't break down now. The ER calls—another injured young man with blood on the floor, an older woman struggling to breathe, loud shouts and quick movements in the trauma bay. She works on autopilot, wearing gloves, starting IVs, hooking up monitors, and speaking calm words with bitten lips.

After the last patient is checked, her body hurts, but she carefully loosens her stiff fingers and texts Mateo: "We'll pay the bills. No matter what. Hang on." She rewrites the message five times before sending it. None say what she really means: Don't give up. Not while I'm here.

The locker room smells of starch and tiredness. She leans on the metal bench, her eyes burning, grief caught in her throat. Memories surface: sneaking into the apartment after night school janitorial jobs, making flashcards for Mateo at midnight while their mother slept. The calendar is full of daily duties. She fights helplessness, pulls back her ponytail, and smooths her face. If anyone sees her cry, they'll think she's weak—not strong with love and fear.

Light rain falls as she steps outside. Puddles scatter across the dark street, neon lights reflecting in broken patterns on the wet pavement. Her rideshare is five minutes away. She unlocks her phone, scrolling through hospital emails—routine stuff: shift sign-ins, badge reminders, flu rules. But some lines stand out—words like "increased watch," "operational changes," and a note about "leadership review policies" for the next board meeting. A memo quietly suggests that staff talk to department heads about "unusual night procedures."

Her heart skips as she recalls Dr. Darius Hale—tense and angry after the failed surgery—and how other surgeons speak in quiet tones when he walks by. She wonders if he feels these changes. She wonders if the Orion Brotherhood's power reaches every corner of St. Gabriel's, and what would happen if the hospital really became a dangerous place. Could Darius—or anyone—stand up against them?

Dawn's blue light makes the steel and glass outside look sharp and strange. Her breath mixes with the faint mist. The hospital is behind her, its windows like empty eyes. Something in the air feels different. She shivers—not from the cold, but from knowing her life teeters on a sharp edge.

She thinks about the numbers she must figure to keep their family going, the talks she avoids with Mateo, and the dark shadow Darius casts. What if Darius falls? Will the corruption spread, pulling more staff into a quiet, secret war?

Her phone buzzes: the car is here. She grips her bag and steps into the pre-dawn quiet. There's no time to hesitate. Both her worlds shake. She straightens her shoulders and walks to the curb, refusing to show fear.

Mid-morning brings silence to the hospital's admin wing, the quiet after a busy night. Lila walks quickly, her sneakers soft on the pale floor, a folder tight against her chest. Doors shine under bright lights—glass with frosted panels hiding talks she won't hear. Most of the hall is empty, cold and bright, smelling of cleaners with a faint hint of coffee in the air.

She pushes open double doors, looking for an empty bathroom. Instead, she slows—voices come through a heavy boardroom door. Light glows beneath it.

"I'm telling you," a woman's voice says sharply—Victoria Grant, clear in her clipped tone, "the Orion plan must be handled quietly. No mistakes."

A low male voice replies, "No one suspects anything. If we act carefully—"

"What about Dr. Hale?" Victoria's voice is cold and sharp. "He's a problem now. I want no questions about loyalty if the review happens."

Lila's skin feels cold. Her grip tightens on the folder. She freezes in the hallway, barely breathing. The administrative air is thinner here than in the ER. A vent hums overhead. Her pulse pounds in her ears.

"The rumors are spreading. The senior staff are asking about him." The man's voice is bored. "We made sure the surgical board will review him. Quietly."

"Keep it that way. If anyone slips, there are already enough accusations. Trusted doctors will be told to question his recent work. Quietly but firmly. We can't have breaks in the team. Old alliances are breaking."

The second voice agrees. "No risk. The Brotherhood depends on secrets, which are never perfect."

Lila hears their words and fights panic. A coup, spoken so plainly. Darius's name, like a knife in their mouths. She sees the bright lights of the operating room, the skilled hands of Darius saving lives others left behind. A man pushed out by politics and suspicion. This is how they attack him—not openly, but by spreading doubt until he stands alone.

Her throat tightens. She closes her eyes, not wanting to see faces she trusted—wondering who is caught in this and who will turn away when the attack comes. She feels angry and guilty—she hasn't done enough and can't do more. Her certainty shakes.

She looks down at the crack under the door and up at the sterile ceiling. It's easy to hide conflict behind rules here. The Brotherhood's power is only strong because it's secret. Power shifts like loose stones in the hospital. In a place of glass and steel, real power is not skill but loyalty, rumors spread quietly from door to door. Alliances form and break before most start their shift. Rival surgical teams seek favor with a nod, a rumor, sometimes deeper conflict. One word, spoken at the right moment in a secret meeting, can build or end a career.

The Orion Brotherhood's shadow is long but not unbreakable. They control votes and policies, but their enemies know how to weaken them: spread doubt, raise questions, and plant poison seeds that grow unseen. The heart of St. Gabriel's beats not just with urgency but with secret wars most staff never see. Today, Lila stands on the edge, more exposed than ever.

Footsteps come from down the hall. Lila pulls back from the door, hiding around the corner. Her breath is fast and sharp. She presses against the wall, praying her heart slows. Her fingers hurt from gripping the folder.

"You'll handle Dr. Ambrose?" Victoria's voice is softer.

"I'll do it."

Heels click, and the door opens. Two calm figures pass down the hall. Lila doesn't move until the silence returns, heavy and dangerous.

She steps out, her vision blurry, her chest tight. Each step feels heavy, like moving underwater with the weight of what she heard. Friends will turn to foes. Darius will be hunted and blamed for invisible failures. Those who support him will share his exile.

At the empty hallway crossing, Lila shakes, her shoulders hunched, her eyes full of shock and anger. She blinks hard, fighting the urge to give up.

She knows now what she heard: the first signs of destruction beneath the surface. It will take more than bravery to survive what's coming.

The cafeteria is loud with bright lights, worn floors, and lunch carts in the corners. Midday hunger makes voices rise, but there is tension beneath every look and laugh. Lila walks in, her scrub pants brushing her ankles, the smell of burnt coffee and bleach sticking in the air. Most people don't notice her, but some watch and whisper.

At the side, Dr. Morris and a surgical resident just off night shift talk quietly but sharply. The resident pokes at cold eggs. "Bet he's out by Friday. Should have been months ago. Dr. Hale's favored status won't save him."

Morris snorts. "Heard it was that last surgery. No one wants to fix Hale's mistakes anymore. Even the board is done pretending he's untouchable." His sneer is fake and oily.

Lila freezes, her hand halfway to a styrofoam cup. The words hit hard, adding to her deep tiredness and heartache. She thinks of Darius—sharp-eyed, precise—alone in the middle of this storm, while others circle like predators. If she walks away, what they want will be the only story left.

She steps forward, coffee forgotten, her footsteps lost in the noise of trays and clatter.

"Dr. Hale isn't perfect." Her voice is calm and steady. "I was there that night. I saw him risk everything to save a patient everyone else gave up on." She sets her jaw as the noise fades. "So before you bet on his failure, remember what this place is supposed to mean."

The table goes quiet. The resident tightens his lips. Morris shrugs, his eyes narrowed but unwilling to meet her gaze. Around them, heads lift. Voices quiet; eyes flicker between Lila and the two men.

Nurse Emma, nearby with her sandwich and chart, puts her food down, cautious but supportive. Junior nurses fidget, looking at Lila with a bit of awe. ICU's Dr. Ishaan gives a small nod—quiet support, nothing bold.

Others pull back, shields up: Dr. Patel and her group move away to a private huddle. Mumbled comments, whispers not meant for ears, but no one defends the gossipers. Alliances, once clear, blur and shift.

The cafeteria smells like failed diets, bitter rivalries, and plastic trays. But today it becomes a hot place where hidden loyalties crack.

Lila stands in the buzz, her heart pounding. Adrenaline fades as her words end. Her hands tremble; she presses them to her sides to hide it.

She remembers the first patient she and Darius saved—a teenager who overdosed, called a "lost cause" by others. Darius sent people rushing for blood, cold fluids, and hope. His angry face that night hid terror and determination—something like courage mixed with guilt. He worked long after others gave up.

No one here knows that. Or that Mateo sits on their old couch, rationing pills because hope costs too much. Most staff won't understand losing your footing or being hunted by rumors.

Talk starts again, slowly then all at once. Old teammates avoid her gaze. True believers, who shared late shifts or jokes, hesitate before quick smiles—some real, some forced. Some bow their heads and pretend she's not there. It hurts but is honest.

"You shouldn't stir things up, Moreno. People don't forget when you choose sides." Morris tries a quiet warning, though his voice shakes.

"Let them remember. Maybe it'll keep others honest."

"Suit yourself. Just don't expect anyone to back you up."

Lila turns away, tasting bitterness. Her fingers shake, but she won't clench them. The double doors creak as she leaves—into the quiet hallway, pale sunlight and faint burnt toast smell from the kitchen.

Her reflection is sharp on the glass. Her jaw is set, her eyes bright with storm. Another battle line is drawn—everyone watching to see if she stands or falls.

She lets the doors close behind her. For now, she won't give in.

The key sticks in the lock—she has to jiggle it before the door opens to a small apartment filled with the soft light of early evening. The air smells of cumin and old wood, with burnt coffee near the kitchen. Quiet fills the rooms—no laughter, no talking—just Mateo slouched on a worn sofa. He's pale, with dark circles under his eyes, surrounded by a pile of mail she dreaded today: hospital letters, a red utility notice, and supermarket flyers sticking out like tongues.

His hoodie is too big, the sleeves covering thin wrists. The TV is on but unseen, casting blue shadows on his face. The familiar weight presses in her chest as she takes off her shoes—too tired from alarms and trauma calls to feel much but this heavy silence.

Mateo doesn't look up until she sits on the coffee table near him. She doesn't need words—her hand finds his, cold and shaking, pushing the mail aside. He looks at the dirt under his nails, his mouth tight like he's hiding something, then finally sighs—a soft, hesitant breath.

"Lila, I—" His voice breaks. "They sent these again. The last test results. I… haven't picked up my medicine. I just didn't want you to know."

She squeezes his hand. "You can't do that. You have to take your meds. We'll find a way."

"I didn't want to make things worse," he says, looking everywhere but at her. "You work so much already, and Mom's barely home, and—"

"Stop." She cuts in, no anger, just firm care. "We'll get through this. Together. Okay?"

He nods but shakes as he rubs his eyes, tears coming.

"I'm scared, Lila. I feel useless. Like you'd be better off if—"

"Don't say that." She moves around the table, pulling him close. His hair is soft under her hand, his breath uneven on her shirt. She holds him tight, trying to press out his fear and shame. She remembers the boy who once slept beside her during storms, holding her hand to feel safe.

He sniffs, "Sorry. Thanks for…"

"You don't have to thank me for being your sister. You're not a burden. None of this is your fault, okay?" She pulls back just enough to look at him in the lamp light. "Some things are worth fighting for. Even when I'm tired, even when it feels impossible. Especially then."

He tries a small smile—old strength in his eyes. She smooths his hair, waiting for his words.

"You always say that. Maybe that's why I keep going," Mateo whispers.

She laughs quietly, rough but real. "Good. Because I'm not letting go. Ever."

He leans back, tired but steadier. She stands and squeezes his knee, her hand lingering a moment, reluctant to leave.

She moves quietly into the kitchen. Every sound counts: mugs clinking, bills sorted neatly, pen scraping as she writes a short note for their mother—"Shift ran late, bills on the table, leftover rice in the fridge. Love, Lila." She cleans the counter, the habit of tidying up the messes her brother and mother miss. She moves fast, protecting herself from pain that still threatens. The cat jumps on the windowsill, tail twitching, watching the dark sky deepen.

She goes through these small routines with steady hands. These simple acts, done with love and defiance, help keep hopelessness away. There were nights when Mateo coughed hard, days counting coins for the bus, times their mother cried over hospital papers she couldn't understand. Through it all, Lila worked harder—extra shifts, reading insurance papers by dim light, helping Mateo study late. These struggles shaped her, making her stronger, less broken. She learned pain isn't just something to suffer—it can make you tougher. She made promises, to herself and Mateo, in times like this: nothing will break them—not bills, illness, or guilt.

She puts on her jacket and bag, kissing Mateo's forehead gently. Her pockets hold receipts and a tangled charger—proof of a life kept together by grit and hope. At the door, she pauses, taking in the small apartment—the chipped table, family photos above the thermostat, the faint echo of happier times. This home is fragile but standing.

She closes the door softly behind her. The night cools around her. The city pulses with distant lights—a restless, hungry thing, promising tough battles ahead. Lila lifts her chin, fear sharp on her tongue, but below it, a familiar strength. She steps into the evening, ready to face whatever comes.

A Fracture in the Ice

Chaos strikes just after midnight—a banshee wail as the ambulance doors crash open, slicing through the hum of St. Gabriel's ER. Fluorescent lights glare against tiled floors, spotlighting two paramedics maneuvering a gurney toward the packed registration desk. On it, a small boy lies limp and impossibly pale, his skin waxy and lips blue. His mother's red eyes gleam with panic as she stumbles to keep pace, fingers twisted around his tiny hand, mouthing hoarse pleas that snag on gasps.

The undercurrent of order dissolves in an instant. Phones ring out unheeded, and the odor of antiseptic mixes with sweat and coffee as nurses rearrange at breakneck speed. A triage nurse—a woman with exhausted eyes—waves furiously to an assembling trauma team.

"Code Blue, pediatric! Clear the next bay!"

Lila shoves aside a rolling chart and squeezes between the circle of frantic adults. Gloved hands already trembling, she threads an IV line into the boy's arm, calling the numbers as they spike and fall beneath her fingertips: "BP eighty over forty. Heart rate one-fifty."

The hospital's soundtrack—beeping monitors, tinny overhead calls, someone sobbing—rises and falls, dense as a thunderstorm.

The boy's mother chokes past the nurses, her voice nearly lost. "Please... he said his tummy hurt, then he just—" She reaches for her son's face, but Lila intercepts her with a look that's both an apology and a command.

"Ma'am, we need space to help him. I'll update you, I promise."

A nurse pages the surgeon—his name is an invocation, a ward against disaster. "Dr. Hale to trauma bay. Dr. Hale, stat."

He arrives as if conjured—Darius Hale in a white coat, his face all knife-edge assurance, shoulders squared against the world. He yanks gloves into place and grabs the chart, scanning it line by line, even as the chaos churns around him. His eyes flick up once, meeting the boy's—a flicker of something softer, a storm kept sternly at bay.

"Sedation and O2, now," he orders, his voice tight, eyes already parsing new threats on the ultrasound. "I want surgical trays prepped. You—" to a sleep-deprived resident, "scan for abdominal bleeding. Tell radiology we need priority access. Lila, you're with me."

The world shrinks to monitors, numbers, sweat. The child whimpers, swallowing air. Darius bends low, his palm gentle on the boy's shoulder, his voice pitched quiet—a practiced cadence that masks all tremors of uncertainty.

"It's all right," he whispers, but his own jaw fractures as he reads the images coming to life on the monitor—a blooming dark mass where there shouldn't be one.

Internal chaos simmers beneath his clinical efficiency. This—this crucible of emergency, of fragile bodies and racing clocks—should call forth only the surgeon's cold, inhuman discipline. But the Brotherhood's creed is little comfort in the white-hot moment before a decision. Control is everything—they've beaten that mantra into his bones. Yet guilt sneaks in, slippered and silent. Long ago, he lost a child's heartbeat to the indifferent hands of time. Is it memory or premonition that needles at him now?

"Let's move!" he barks. The team leaps to obey. Hands—his, Lila's, the resident's—lift the boy to a waiting gurney. He weighs nothing, a bundle of bones, and his mother's cries recede. Darius propels the gurney down the hall, barking to the anesthesiologist and surgical nurse as they align at the OR doors.

"Type and cross. Forty mils of blood, two units prepped. Page pediatric anesthesia." Every word is measured, a scaffolding—keep busy, keep moving, don't let it in.

The operating suite draws them into a world of gleaming metal and chilling light. The air here is so clean it almost burns, humming with ozone and recent sterilization. Hands scrubbed raw, Lila and Darius stand shoulder to shoulder as the others flit and fade behind masks.

Scalpel. Skin. The first incision spills crimson onto the blue drape. Someone tenses, but Darius's hands don't betray the lurch in his mind: years ago, another tiny body, another room, another night. Accusations echo from the past—parents' cries, Caius's measured disappointment, the Brotherhood's silent council. Not now. Not again.

"Vessel. Clamp." He speaks around the hot spark of fear, his voice the axis on which the room turns.

The monitors shriek in electronic distress. Lila wipes sweat from his brow with the edge of her sleeve. Darius leans into the steady blip of the child's remaining heartbeat, his own pulse a frantic drum in his ears.

"You're safe," he breathes, more for himself than the child as he stitches mess to order, reining chaos into narrow seams. The surgery bleeds minutes and hours.

A sigh ripples through the team as readings steady—bleeding staunched, heartbeat a strong, golden line. Lila's gloved hand squeezes Darius's shoulder, the only praise he'll allow.

"You did it," she says, her voice salt-soft, eyes shining with relief.

He lingers a beat longer, fingers still wrapped around the boy's hand, as if afraid to let him slip away. Something inside—too hard, too long—is breaking, just a little. The shielded surgeon, caught in the act of hope.

Then he releases the child, and the room, all color and sound and ache, blurs behind him as he walks out in silence, leaving fragments of himself stitched among the sutures.

Darius slips through the corridor, shoulders squared, his face expressionless under the harsh LED glare. The world of St. Gabriel's has always turned briskly, but after the hurricane of the emergency room, its churn now feels off-kilter, agitated. Nurses drift past in blue scrubs, glancing at him with curiosity barely concealed. Darius walks faster, his shoes silent on the recently mopped linoleum, turning corners with swift calculation until he reaches an almost hidden lounge. An old sign, half-peeled from the door. He pushes inside.

Inside, the light is dim, the only illumination a jaundiced rectangle leaking from a crack under the door, and the pale silver of fluorescent bulbs overhead. Vending machines blink along the far wall with sullen, artificial colors. A battered leather couch sits in the center, its upholstery cracked and faded, the seams split and stuffing poking out near one arm. Darius sits heavily, elbows dropping to his knees, head sinking into his hands. The clangor of the hospital recedes—voices, code calls, footsteps—rendered distant, as if submerged underwater. He hears only the distant shudder of a rattling gurney and the sleepy hum of the soda machine, cycling air through sticky innards. The scent in here is equal parts plastic, sweat, and a faint stale packet of instant coffee, forgotten on a side table.

Darkness angles over Darius's shoulders, heavy and certain. He presses the heels of his hands against his eyes. Behind his eyelids, the boy's white, frightened face springs up—motionless, bloodless, the sharp lines of collarbones beneath too-loose hospital cotton. His own hands are shaking, he realizes now, even as a ghost memory—gloved, steady, precise—replays in the operating suite. The weight of failure presses old bruises into new skin.

He remembers the Brotherhood's private dining room: a polished cherry wood table so glossy it reflected city lights, the air thick with the smell of leather and polished brass. Caius stands beside him, the old mentor's hand a steady anchor on his shoulder. In the hush broken only by the clink of glasses, Caius says, "We all break, but never in public. Control is survival." Words spoken low, for their ears only—iron forged from decades of unbending discipline and brutal, necessary secrecy. Darius has carried the doctrine ever since, letting it tunnel through his bones until composure became his armor, silence his mask.

But that armor doesn't hold tonight. Images from the operating room claw through the chinks: the child's labored breathing, his mother's pleas turned keening whimpers at the door. Under the fierce white sting of surgical light, Darius's hands had not hesitated—scalpel, clamp, suture, a choreography rehearsed so often the body remembers when the mind frays. Yet afterward, a cold sweat had broken out at his temples, and his chest still aches with the fading echo of fight-or-flight. The worst part is how familiar it all is—the flash of failure, a small patient's pulses slackening beneath his hands, memories cracking through the sterile ritual of surgery.

Darius clenches his fists, nails biting half-moons into his palms. Control. Always, for the Brotherhood, for the hospital, for the ghosts who never quite leave. His own past mistakes—failings whispered behind closed doors—have carved deeper channels than any lesson learned in a classroom. The Brotherhood's shadow is long, its expectations heavier than the city skyline itself. Weakness, once, brought questions. Three months ago, a tragedy in this very hospital—one error, one child lost, headlines that threatened to unravel everything he was. Since then, Darius has been ice on the surface, meticulous, unyielding, the kind of man whose reputation is his only shield. Loose threads get tugged, and his world could come undone.

He wonders, in this dimly lit cocoon, whether the control he's worshipped has only imprisoned him. He can still recall the trembling in his fingers as they stitched rupture after rupture. A surgeon's hands aren't supposed to shake. When they do, people die. That simple. And if people die, what good is all the Brotherhood's power and secrecy—what can it protect? The hospital's walls may be glass and steel, spotless and modern, but inside him, guilt sits like rot beneath a polished floor, dull and gnawing. He tells himself it's only exhaustion. He doesn't believe it.

For a moment, the world thins to the faint tick of a wall clock, the acid scent of hand sanitizer, the flickering shadows that collect in the lounge's corners. Darius's thoughts soup and clot, grasping at old lessons. Strength means never showing what's broken. There are things you confess only to darkness and the silent, humming vending machines. Caius would say control is the only thing more precious than reputation. But what about connection? What about mercy for yourself?

Regret expands in his chest, sharp-edged, invasive, threatening the rigor mortis of composure that has defined his nights. The fortress he's built feels paper-thin. He fights the urge to break down, swallowing it, breathing in the chemical-tinged air. His breath shakes anyway. Tonight, secrecy is a scarf too tightly knotted, and discipline feels like a chokehold.

His head tips back against the worn couch, eyes drifting shut. The tension in his jaw slackens. A fraught exhale slips past his lips—shaky, audible in the hush. For this breath, at least, Darius Hale is not the world-renowned surgeon or the Brotherhood's stoic perfectionist. He is just a man, exhausted and unspeakably alone, his vulnerability filling the room for once, unhidden.

Lila stands just beyond the threshold, the battered staff lounge drenched in gray shadows and dusted with the faintest glow from a grimy vending machine screen. The cinder block walls leak the day's cold into her skin, and her arms tighten around herself as if she could wring out the memory of shrieking monitors and blood. Darius occupies the far end of the cracked couch, his tall form distilled into planes of tension—a man carved from stone, but tonight, edges softening into exhaustion. His elbows press into his knees, his face hidden behind pale hands, every line of his body saying, *don't come closer*. Still, Lila doesn't retreat.

She studies him quietly, the drum of her heartbeat loud in this thin hush. The air in here is thick with the smell of old coffee, disinfectant, and something older—a scent of sleepless hope, maybe. Everything she's seen of him until now—a surgeon's icy discipline, that glacial barked authority—slips away. He seems terribly human under the sickly flicker of overhead bulbs. For a moment, she remembers herself: the girl dragged awake by ambulance sirens in the Texas dawn, always strong for her brother, never bending. She recognizes him in that posture—a different kind of fortress, but built for the same reason.

Lila doesn't speak right away. She walks in, letting the battered door whoosh shut behind her, her kneecaps bumping the low table as she sits at his side. The old vinyl groans beneath her, the space between them buzzing with what neither will say. She's close enough now to see a faint tremor in his hand, the precise surgeon's touch betrayed by the smallest quake.

"Hey," she says quietly, searching his profile. "Is it—are you all right?"

Darius drags one hand down his face. Under his fingers, she glimpses the weary angle of his jaw, that thin scar catching the artificial light. His reply nearly dissolves into the stale air.

"I'm not sure," he murmurs. "That case—the boy. It's... it shouldn't get to me, but it does. Sometimes I think I've learned how to lock it out." The words slide reluctantly from him. "But tonight, I couldn't."

He falls silent, a man struggling to keep every splintered piece inside. His eyes, always distant, blink with an ache she recognizes from her own mirror. Regret, old and sharp, etches lines down his face.

She listens, her hands loose in her lap, careful not to startle his vulnerability into hiding. There's something sacred in this, she thinks—a small admission between warriors just off the battlefield. Lila's voice is low, nearly lost behind the heater's hum.

"I get it," she tells him. "I used to think the longer I worked here, the less families would haunt me. But they do. Every single one." She tangles her fingers, thinking of all the kids she's lost, the mothers who've clutched her scrubs the way she clutches paychecks at home. "Sometimes I go home after a shift and can't even talk to Mateo. My brother. But the loneliness inside these walls..." She breathes in shallowly, the words tasting of ten years' ache. "It's heavy. Even outside."

His surprise isn't dramatic—just the small tilt of his head, a tightening at the corners of his eyes. Empathy, or confusion at her honesty, she can't tell. It's enough, though, for him to meet her gaze fully for the first time—not as the ice surgeon, nor the silent judge, but as another soul scraping through these midnight corridors.

"Thank you," he says, and the ice in his tone is gone—what replaces it is soft, bruised, and tentative. "For not pretending. For listening."

They fall into a gentle quiet, letting the hospital's background noise drift over them: the whining of distant machines, a nurse's laughter caught down the hall, the soft growls of their own exhaustion. Lila's hand hovers, indecisive, before resting over his—not a declaration, but a quiet offering. Her thumb brushes once against his skin, as if reminding him he's more than the man weighed down by failure.

The moment holds, breathless and fragile. The heater rattles on, pushing out its metallic warmth. She closes her eyes, feeling the boundary between them dissolve—not completely, but enough for hope to slip through a crack.

Light above them shudders, casting their shadows in uneven stripes across the floor. From the hallway, footsteps and the muffled whir of a rolling cart intrude. A nurse passes by, her silhouette slicing the glass panel near the door, and their bubble of dusk and candor wavers. Still, Lila doesn't move her hand, and Darius, for once, doesn't draw away. There's a new charge in the air—the start of trust, the brittle sweetness of connection raw and recent.

When the noises retreat and the hall falls silent again, something wordless has rooted between them. For tonight, the spirits of fear and old wounds shrink under the glow of fragile kinship. Lila lets herself hope, just a little, that sometimes, even inside St. Gabriel's labyrinth, the cold can be kept at bay.

Stolen Breaks

The hum of the vending machine and the faint whir of overhead lights are the only sounds in the staff lounge, a glass cage suspended between night and day. It still smells faintly of burnt coffee and disinfectant, layered over by the metallic tang of adrenaline that lingers after every crisis. A plastic clock on the wall clicks just loud enough to mark time but not quite loud enough to invade the moment.

Lila sits sprawled in a battered armchair, the heels of her sneakers propped on the low table—her posture a direct challenge to the professional decorum of St. Gabriel's. She cradles a steaming mug and peeks over the rim, her eyes settling on the overstuffed planner balanced with almost surgical precision on Darius's lap.

She lets out a soft, deliberate sigh and bites into the silence. "You realize you look like the billionaire surgeon who never laughs, right? Is that planner full of stock prices, or do you actually schedule time to frown at people?" Her voice is teasing, light, almost daring him.

Darius does not immediately turn toward her. He sits upright—too upright—on the edge of the cracked vinyl couch, a pen clamped precisely between his fingers. The pages of his planner are lined with blocks of color and precise notations, transformed into a battlefield where nothing is left to chance. His eyes, cold and steel gray, flicker up to meet hers. For a moment, his expression remains inscrutable marble, the mask he's worn through every loss, every suspicion, and every whispered rumor that clings to the sterile corridors beyond these walls.

But then the corner of his mouth betrays him. The faintest tug, barely a breath of movement—a smile, fighting its way free.

Lila sets her mug down with a soft clink. She grins, savoring the breach in his defenses. "Be honest. Do you wake up at 5:00 every morning just to alphabetize your tie collection by hue? Are your socks organized by occasion, or do you just have a drawer labeled 'soul-crushingly serious'?"

Darius sets the planner aside—hesitation in the unpracticed motion, as though he's relinquishing a shield—and lets out a sound. It starts as a huff but dissolves into something abrupt and genuine. A chuckle, deep and low, vibrating through the hollow quiet of the lounge. It's a sound out of place here, where laughter usually dies swiftly or is muffled behind closed doors.

Lila's eyes widen, delight quick and bright. "Did you just—? Oh God. Stop the presses. Darius Hale is capable of laughter."

He lifts his chin, still composed, but another smile ghosts across his features, a fleeting warmth.

"What, do you want evidence?" he says, almost—almost—deadpan, but softer at the edges. "I suppose you'll want something scandalous next. For your records."

She leans in, elbows on her knees, all mischief. "Obviously. I can't go back to Emma and say we talked about surgical technique. Give me a secret. Something that would scandalize the Brotherhood."

His eyes drop to the planner as if searching it for escape, but her voice—its honesty, its heat—holds him in place. He sighs. "I was twelve. Prep school. They caught me—"

He hesitates, glances up, and seems to weigh the risk of telling her the story at all.

"I put a frog in the headmaster's office. Under his chair. It croaked during morning prayers. I got a week's detention."

There is a beat of silence as the confession hovers, improbably weightless and absurd in his mouth.

Lila's expression is priceless—mock outrage, eyebrows arched high. "A frog? I'm shocked. Next, you'll tell me you used to doodle in the margins, too."

He shrugs, a gesture at once defensive and sheepish. "My artistic career was short-lived. I stuck to anatomy sketches. Less incriminating."

Her laughter erupts, free and full, and he lets it fill the stale air between them. The clinical white lights are soft for a moment, gentled by the sound.

"You," she says between peals, "are far more dangerous than you let on, Dr. Hale." She wipes an imaginary tear from the corner of her eye, her lips quirking into a crooked, playful smile.

He lets himself relax, the tension coiled in his shoulders melting just enough that he almost forgets the weight of expectation, the memory of blood on gloved hands, and voices whispering in the halls. For a too-brief span, the world is only the two of them in this outdated lounge, an island of nearly human peace.

Lila's gaze lingers, and he can feel the lines between them blur—her warmth coaxing color back into his guarded world.

"Is this the part where I find out you've secretly got a pet tarantula?" she says, her voice a tease but her eyes too soft to mock.

He shakes his head, a rueful smile lingering. "Only the frog, I'm afraid."

The laughter lingers after their voices fade, humming softly with the vending machine, as if the walls themselves know this moment is rare. For a heartbeat, peace breathes between them, fragile and bright as dawn.

Darius rises from his chair, his movements deliberate and precise, a notebook pressed tight against his side as if it could anchor him to the world. He offers Lila a wordless flick of his head, the barest invitation to follow. The lounge door sighs shut behind them. The corridor beyond is half-lit, shadows stretching long between sickly, buzzing bulbs. Though midnight lingers, the heart of the hospital is electric with residual energy: the faint hum of ventilation, a clipped radio broadcast echoing from a distant nurse's station, and footsteps swallowed quickly by the labyrinth of tile.

Darius leads her right, slipping into a back hallway—the one behind the operating rooms, rarely used, silent as a crypt. The air here is heavy with the tang of sterile wipes and cooled metallic hints. Lila's sneakers scuff against the institutional floor; Darius's shoes make barely a sound. He stops, pressing his shoulders back against the chilled wall. Pale-green paint is flaking along the baseboards. His breath fogs faintly, dissipating beneath the flicker of the fluorescents.

He doesn't speak at first. He studies the mottled ceiling, his jaw tight, lines of exhaustion and something keener carved deep into his face. Darius, the surgeon known for unswerving focus, seems to fight himself in this silence, chiseling away at whatever remains of his composure.

"I thought I could be perfect for them," Darius says, his voice flat but brittle at the edges, his eyes locked on the black seam between two wall tiles. "That if I never slipped, if I played the role—brotherhood's golden boy—they'd never see the flaws." His gaze drifts, the memory of error sharp as alcohol in an open wound. "The night it happened... I lost a patient. Not even medicine, not the Brotherhood's poison, could save them. Afterward—" his throat constricts, "—I kept thinking, if I'd been more vigilant, less human, maybe—"

A filament in the fixture above them sputters, casting Darius's face in broken relief. Shadows swallow half his expression, the other lit cold and white. He closes his eyes, as if the flickering light needles through old scars beneath his skin. The wordless ache of expectation presses against him—every whispered command from the elders, every sidelong glance after the tragedy. What they ask of him feels as heavy as the world and twice as lonely.

Lila hugs herself, retreating to the opposite wall. The distance between them is less than a stretcher's width, but it feels like a chasm built from the things left unsaid. She lets out a breath that shakes, breath scented with hospital coffee lingering on her lips. Her eyes track Darius, searching for the man beneath the armor.

"Sometimes I think if I just work hard enough... maybe everything falls into place," she murmurs, her voice thin. "But the bills keep coming. My brother keeps needing. And my family looks at me like I'm supposed to have the answers. I smile for them. I hold it together. Because if I don't, it falls apart." She laughs, a soft sound, something between despair and defiance. "Most nights, I lie awake measuring what the world will take from us next. And I'm so damn tired of pretending I've got it covered."

A silent beat stretches the air tight. The corridor seems to hold its breath, the distant click and whir of hospital machinery the only reminder that the building is alive.

Lila's hand trembles where her fingers clutch her elbows. "You know what scares me?" She looks up, the emergency exit sign boring a limp red glow above her head. "That one little mistake... not even a big one, could be the thing that ruins us. I'm always right at the edge, waiting for that last shove."

Darius lifts his gaze. The sharpness in his eyes is tempered now, his gaze softer. "I envy that you can say it. That you let yourself feel all of it, even with the world watching." His voice is rough-edged with longing, almost reverent.

She snorts. "Yeah, well. It feels less brave at three in the morning when you're ugly-crying into your pillowcase."

He manages something close to a smile, his shoulders falling back as the grip on his planner loosens. They stand, mirrors to each other's wounds, each recognizing the web of duty and worry etched into the other's features.

"It's strange," Darius murmurs, "how pressure can hollow you out. I spend all day holding everything together. But there's nothing left for me when the theater is empty. Nothing but... fractures." He shrugs. "Still, your honesty—there's strength in it."

Lila's head tilts, her hair falling loose from her bun. Her words come gentle, shaped by fatigue and something like hope. "I think you're steadier than you know. Even if you don't talk about it. Even if you're scared you'll unravel."

Their gazes cling, silent understanding rising like heat from the sterile tile. In this faint, artificial light, with exhaustion muddying the boundaries and old shame stripped bare, their burdens twine together, neither heavier nor lighter, but shared.

Lila steps closer, reaching out. Her fingertips rest lightly against Darius's forearm—solid and strong beneath sleeve and skin, but trembling. The gesture is small, impossibly tender against hospital coldness.

"You don't have to be perfect here," she whispers.

Darius's features relax, the lines of tension softening with her touch. For the first time all night, the anxiety ringing through his chest eases, just enough. The world outside—the rumors, the obligations, the ghosts—recedes for a beat, replaced by the hush of breathing and the faraway lull of the ward. The corridor holds their secrets in the hum of machinery and distant alarms, a fragile peace hanging in the air, breaking open the possibility that maybe, just maybe, neither of them is alone.

Darius and Lila move side by side out of the silent, slender corridor. The hush of the hospital at this hour feels alien, the hum of faraway machines the only note in a muffled symphony. A harsh strip of overhead lights splays pale shadows on the scuffed tile, rendering them twin silhouettes crossing into the wide, empty hallway. Their footsteps are muted and rhythmic, the air thick with the residue of truths confessed minutes before.

They are inches apart—closer, somehow, than the physical gap allows. As they near the nurses' station, their hands swing almost in unison. Lila feels the edge of Darius's knuckle graze her skin. The contact is featherlight, but it sears—her pulse leaps, heat racing through her torso. Her fingers twitch, unsteady, and her shoes squeak to an abrupt halt. Darius stops, too, breath catching audibly in the dim.

She glances up, seeking his eyes, and finds his gaze locked fiercely on her. Everything in the background fades—the gurneys, the antiseptic tang, the cold geometry of walls—all dwarfed by the gravity in his stare. In this moment, two people exist in opposition to the rest of the world, secret and bared. She sees herself reflected in obsidian: strong, scared, wanting.

Neither of them speaks. The silence grows ripe. Lila senses electricity sweeping through her body. She watches the way Darius stands—rigid spine, jaw tense, his throat tight—and sees a tremor in his composure. His lips, usually set and measured, part by a breath. She could count the milliseconds they hover here, hearts volleying, the night's earlier laughter reborn as something fragile and dangerous.

Lila lets the smallest smile break. Slow, deliberate, it curls at the corners of her mouth—an invitation; a dare. Without a word, she tips her chin up and waits. Darius's eyes flick down to her lips. He doesn't move forward but doesn't retreat. They hover on the threshold, their joined shadows stretching across the floor.

Darius's hand falls open at his side, and he holds her gaze for a heartbeat longer than is wise. The air between them hums with unspoken want—something reckless and forbidden pressing just beneath his neatly starched shirt, beneath all his rules. The promise glistens: there could be more, if only the world would let them.

In the far end of the hall, footsteps echo—a nurse, maybe, or early-morning cleaning staff. The spell quivers. Darius flinches, his eyes sharpening. He tears his gaze from hers, his face shuttering, as though a curtain drops between them. The faintest flush creeps up his throat—a secret blooming in hostile soil.

"I should..." He checks his watch, his voice a low rasp as he drags order back into himself. "...patients are waiting." His hand curls into a fist, the tremor barely contained. He puts a measured stride between them, feigning composure as he squares his shoulders, every muscle taut.

Lila doesn't follow, not yet. She remains stationary, her heart still thudding where their skin had touched. The fluorescent glow frames

Darius's retreat, every step deliberate, as if distance could erase what just passed between them. She watches, silent, as he disappears around the corner, a solitary figure dissolving into the noise and necessity of morning.

Only then does she exhale. Her palm closes over her wrist, tracing the spot where the shock of his hand still lingers—a heat reluctant to fade. The air around her seems changed, as if charged with hidden light. She feels the weight of what lies beneath her steady exteriors—the ache of want, the high-wire tremor of hope, the threat of exposure.

The hospital at dawn is a strange beast: half-asleep, on the verge of waking. Pale sunlight seeps through the atrium's high glass, washing the world in soft promise. Lila stands transfixed, a nurse in battered sneakers, her reflection warped in the sterile shine of the floor. For one impossible second, she imagines: What if she reached for him next time? What if he let her? She sees possible futures collapse and unfurl—quiet mornings, hands entwined, new scars and old secrets mending side by side. Would love loosen something in his haunted heart—or tear her own in half? Could she balance devotion to her family and this unruly need?

She chases the memory of his smile, small and real, tucked into those early-morning shadows. How dangerous to crave the touch of someone bound in a brotherhood of silence. How dangerous to hope he might crave her back just as fiercely.

There's risk in every choice that clicks through her mind: her brother's bills, Darius's glacial isolation, the sharp looks of staff who already whisper. But in the corridor's hush, all that fear sharpens into a slender promise—a dare to step closer, believe in possibility, even if it might not last.

In the distance, the hospital murmurs awake. Lila lowers her hand, steadying her breath, feeling the galaxy of their charged encounter pulse in her blood. Whatever storm waits beyond the next door, she will carry this moment—the jolt, the warmth, the secret smile—into the day ahead, and maybe, into something bigger than either of them can name.

The Rumor Mill

Even before noon, the staff lounge at St. Gabriel's Hospital is filled with the quiet sounds of beeping pagers, humming vending machines, and footsteps echoing down shiny hallways. The air smells of reheated coffee and strong disinfectant. Emma Hayes opens the door, feeling the cold metal handle. At the vending machine, two nurses whisper behind disposable coffee cups, their faces lit by the blue light of the snack screen. When Emma approaches, their voices stop—a silent warning.

One nurse gives a weak smile that doesn't reach her eyes and mentions a missing supply, but she looks at Emma sideways, judging whether she can be trusted or is a threat. Trust here is rare and hard to maintain. Emma feels tense, not from worry, but from the rumors buzzing through the room like static. Gossip never really dies here; it just changes form.

Across the hall, office staff gather by the elevators. Their clicking heels and strong perfume feel out of place among the hospital's usual chaos, but their voices are just as loud as the nurses'. "Can you believe he's still in surgery?" one woman asks, glancing nervously down the hall. "He's untouchable—everyone protects him. The board practically obeys him."

"Yeah, until he makes a big enough mistake," another says quietly. "Money here doesn't just buy silence. It changes the story." Their careful words show they're used to fear. Rumors protect people from those in power and can destroy them when they slip up.

Nearby, the supply closet is cramped with cleaning tools and smells strongly of bleach. Two orderlies argue in both Spanish and English, their faces red with anger. "You think it's just a mistake?" one says, frustrated. "Look who signs the checks. They won't let this leak. My cousin worked in records—he saw files disappear." He snaps his fingers sharply.

The other shakes his head, filling a crowded cart with gloves. "We're all easily replaced, but they aren't. Shadowy donors, favors, hush money—they'll protect themselves. Remember last year's data breach? You forgot that?"

Even in the closet's dull light, fear either brings people together or tears them apart. Information helps but can also hurt. Rumors are something they all share, partly believing and partly afraid.

Near the nurses' station, Dr. Sebastian Crowe talks with Dr. Patel. Their white coats cast long shadows, and their conversation is sharp and indirect. Dr. Patel looks toward the lounge, speaking quietly. "Another scandal will disappear like the last one. The right people can erase it."

Dr. Crowe smirks. "For now, Patel. Power covers a lot, but protection bought with old money doesn't last forever." Their words hang in the air like a warning.

Emma watches from behind a pile of charts, feeling a knot tighten in her stomach. She thinks of Lila—her strong spirit and warm hands—and wishes she could lock all these rumors away. The hospital feels heavy with tension; every glance feels like a warning or an accusation.

In the break room, Lila Moreno steps into the harsh light, the smell of burnt coffee mixed with lemon cleaner. She moves with focus, pouring fresh coffee into a chipped mug. Nearby, two medical residents talk quietly, their words sudden and sharp.

"One mistake and he becomes public enemy number one?"

"That's not it. Powerful donors want him gone. He's made too many enemies—someone wants him out."

Lila stands firm, gripping her cup as if its warmth can fight the cold spreading through her.

"Tell that to his supporters. They'd rather hide the scandal than have the board look bad."

"I'm just saying—be careful. Here, causing trouble gets you crushed."

Lila tightens her jaw, lifts her chin, and walks away, her eyes flicking around.

In the hospital halls, suspicion grows everywhere. St. Gabriel's is built on weak foundations, with rumors acting as both glue and explosives. Truth changes constantly, and friendships form and break as quickly as whispers pass under doors. No one knows where the Brotherhood's power ends and the hospital's begins.

Lila passes Emma with a simple nod, a brief shared moment of tiredness. Holding her cooling coffee, Lila walks down the long, cold hall. The buzz of gossip follows her. Every half-hidden look presses closer, making the hospital feel like it hums with secrets and threats.

Late afternoon sunlight shines between city buildings, but inside Dr. Sebastian Crowe's office, the room is dark. He closes the blinds one slat at a time, blocking out the outside noise. The air smells of wood, paper, disinfectant, sweat, stale coffee, and stress. Crowe stands still, watching the hall. Only the ticking of a clock can be heard. In his mind, he's already planning.

Dr. Patel stands near the door, his coat collar damp. Crowe closes and locks the door, cutting off any warmth from the daylight. He doesn't need to see Patel's nervous face to know he's worried. Patel holds a folder tightly to his chest. His eyes wander from a diploma to a plaque honoring the Brotherhood's donors—a symbol that can both help and threaten them.

Crowe walks behind his desk, standing straight. He runs a finger along the desk and pauses at a gold letter opener, as if considering which tool he'll need—a precise scalpel or a heavy club. "Time is running out," he says quietly but firmly. "The board wants results. I want results. We need to do this quickly and cleanly."

Patel fidgets with the folder. "Are you sure this won't backfire on us?"

Crowe smiles slightly. "I ask the questions; you help find the answers. First, get every record—notes, signed consent forms, operation logs for the past year. If he missed even one witnessed signature, we make a pattern of it. Not a mistake. A pattern."

"Even if—he's only human—" Patel stammers.

Crowe leans over the desk, making himself look bigger. "One mistake can be forgiven. But a series of mistakes? That's not carelessness. That's decay. That's how we make the case."

Patel swallows, then nods. He pulls out marked emails, highlighted nervously. "Victoria Grant and the board want proof, not just rumors. We give them just enough to start doubting, but not enough to trace back to us."

Crowe's eyes shine. "You're learning," he says, half praising, half mocking.

Patel sits, sweating as he reads the pages again. "What if there's an audit? What about his supporters? Drake, Blackwell—"

Crowe stops him with a look, then moves to the window. He opens the blinds slightly and looks out at the street below. Cars move in the sun, unaware of what's happening above. He imagines a changed St. Gabriel's—offices free of Brotherhood members, the hospital controlled by him.

He's waited for this moment. Darius Hale is untouchable now, but his fall will change everything. Crowe almost tastes the fresh, clean power that could wipe out the old greed and secrets. He pictures a boardroom with Victoria's fake smile, Patel's nervousness, himself leading new allies and outside forces ready to act. He knows the risk is high; a mistake could ruin everything. Still, it's worth it for the hospital's future and his own.

He closes the blinds and sits, folding his hands carefully. "The Harper firm is watching. If we shake things enough, they'll help—with money, lawyers, whatever. But only after Darius is weakened."

Patel looks pale, glancing between emails and Crowe. "I understand. We'll start tonight."

Crowe's voice is soft but firm. "Don't think—just act. This isn't about Hale alone. The Brotherhood creates weaknesses. It's time to face the truth."

Patel stands, tense, gathers his folder, and walks out, pausing before he leaves. He looks back, scared but resigned.

Crowe locks the door again, straightens the donor plaque, and wipes it clean. His smile shows no warmth.

The fifth-floor hallway is lit by dull, flickering lights. The air feels heavy and still. Lila's footsteps echo loudly on the worn floor tiles. Somewhere behind a closed door, a phone rings, but no one answers.

Two young nurses stop talking when they see her. One fixes her ponytail, and the other adjusts her scrubs, avoiding eye contact. Lila walks by, standing straight and keeping her hands in her sleeves. Their silence feels heavy, like the smell of hospital cleaner in the air.

She stops by the window near the stairwell. A group of night-shift technicians stands nearby, their faces lit by phone screens. Their voices float under the door—quiet but sharp.

"Did you see Moreno cover for him again? Brave."

"I'd rather hurt myself than get tangled with surgeons like Hale. Nurses helping rich surgeons always get burned."

They laugh, the sound bouncing off the walls, empty and hungry.

"Being in Darius's group has perks, but everything has a price."

Someone makes a slicing gesture with their hand like a knife. Another whispers, "Money cleans messes, but blood leaves stains."

Lila steps back, her heart pounding. The glass stairwell fogs with the memory of many whispered troubles. She forces herself to keep walking, the voices stinging behind her as she heads to the lockers.

She sits on a bench. It creaks under her weight. The air feels cold and stale, like the rest of the night shift has left. From her bag, she takes out her phone; the battery is almost dead. The locker smells like old cloth and lemon oil. She puts her badge in her pocket and reads a memo taped there:

TO ALL STAFF—Donor privacy is a top priority. Any breach of confidentiality will lead to immediate punishment. Administration.

A sick feeling grows in her stomach. Maybe rumors have always been here, but now they want to touch people. She's been careful—never saying names, never leaving texts—but silence feeds suspicion better than truth. She closes her eyes and counts her breaths, imagining how far the Brotherhood's power really goes—beyond Darius's ruined name, beyond her badge. Into the bones of anyone who gets too close.

Was this ever just one mistake? Or was the decision made already in some locked office with a plaque and a gold pen? She pictures eyes watching from upstairs—faces she's never seen. Donors, board members, men who move quiet money and erase what can't be fixed. Even her careful steps leave her exposed, nerves stretched thin. Every kind word, every small act, can be used against her. The memo doesn't name the Brotherhood, but their shadow darkens each line, full of sharp teeth and waiting.

The locker door slams behind her, making her jump.

"Lila." Nurse Cynthia Ramirez's voice is low, urgent, and full of regret. "Can I talk to you?"

Lila checks her pocket for her badge and measures the distance between them.

"Yeah, I'm leaving soon, but—what's up?"

Cynthia looks down the empty room, her voice soft. "Be careful. This whole thing is getting dangerous. Don't let his problems become yours. People are talking—and they aren't just blaming the surgeons anymore."

Lila stiffens. "Are you warning me or threatening me?"

Cynthia swallows, her eyes tired. "I don't want to see you caught in the crossfire. They protect their own; the rest of us? Not so much."

"Maybe you should stop listening to rumors, Cynthia. You know me better."

Cynthia shrugs, defensive. "Doesn't matter what I think. If you fight someone else's fight here, you'll bleed for it sooner or later."

"Maybe someone has to. Maybe I'm okay with that."

"That won't save him. Or you."

Cynthia steps back, looking toward the hall. "Don't say I didn't warn you."

She leaves—white shoes disappearing under the bright lights. Lila exhales, pressing her palm against the cool locker door. She breathes in the sharp smells of dust and sweat.

The weight in her chest stays tight like piano wire. Loyalty tastes strange—bittersweet and full of fear. The hospital isn't just hallways and procedures; it's a creature that eats secrets, spits out bones, and rewrites rules in invisible ink. If she walks away now, she gives up Darius—to boardroom vultures and the unseen Brotherhood's punishment. But standing firm means inviting rumors and suspicion into her life, her job record, and her family's fragile future.

Still, she knows how much fear she can handle. It sharpens her focus and fuels her resolve. She stands tall, closes her locker, and stares at her shadow stretched thin on the floor.

She walks, steady and sure, toward the soft light by the operating rooms. Her footsteps echo in the quiet. When she opens the stairwell door, warm light spills across the metal stairs.

Her steps ring out alone in the quiet. The air is cold against the fire in her spine. The hospital wraps her in twilight and silence, but she keeps moving forward, her fear tight, and her promise to Darius steady and strong.

An Unexpected Rescue

The conference room pulses with barely concealed urgency, every seat around the long, polished table weighed down by the tension brought in by white coats and the chemical scent of sanitizer clinging to the air. Beneath the hum of the overhead lights, nurses and doctors eye each other with practiced wariness, their voices pitched to a hush just above the shuffle of forms and the quiet click of pens against folders. Someone coughs, sharp and dry. Secrets always move fastest in these halls, and today, every glance and mutter circles back to the same name: Darius Hale.

The true gravity of the hospital doesn't reside in the walls or blinking monitors—it seeps from the invisible scaffolding built by donors whose names are etched in gold on distant plaques and from the watchful stares of administrators who decide, behind closed doors, which mistakes are forgivable. The click of stiletto heels and the murmur of authority fill the room as Victoria Grant, in her tailored suit and crisp composure, settles at the head of the table, a folder balanced neatly in her hands. Power reveals itself in posture here—backs straight as boards, every nod measured, every hint of dissension absorbed and filed away for later use.

Lila Moreno slides into her seat, surrounded by murmurs and the faint scent of burnt coffee. The skin along her arms prickles; she feels, with a kind of sixth sense, how hierarchy arranges itself even before the meeting begins. An unspoken contract: those with the right funding or pedigree walk these halls, shielded by invisible armor. The rest tread lightly. In her years as a nurse, she has learned the rhythm—when to blend into the crowd, when to speak. Today, something in her chest presses outward, refusing to sink.

Dr. Sebastian Crowe is the first to stand, the scrape of his chair deliberate as a warning. His hands, clean and steady, rest just inside his jacket before he speaks. His words are scalpel-sharp, cutting into the hush.

"I believe the board—and our staff—deserves real answers regarding Dr. Hale's recent surgical... misjudgments. We're all aware of what's been swirling through the wards. Not every mishap warrants such leniency unless, of course, some of us are just privileged enough to have friends in high places."

His gaze never lands fully on Darius, instead sweeping the room, daring anyone to challenge the narrative he has spun from threads of rumor and envy. People look away, retreating behind neutral expressions, but the implications hang in the fluorescent air, twisting tighter with each breath.

Victoria Grant unclasps her folder, the snap loud enough to silence a side conversation. There's no warmth in her eyes, just calculation simmering beneath her green irises as she addresses the room—her voice brisk, controlled, and carrying the authority of someone accustomed to getting her way.

"We've all seen the donor numbers. And we've all heard about special favors, hush-hush meetings behind closed doors. Where's the transparency? Now, there are whispers—unconfirmed, not yet investigated, but loud enough to threaten our hospital's reputation. Are we prepared to say merit alone protects our staff, or has influence bought immunity?"

Her measured words lodge like splinters in the room. Lila sees Victoria's gaze rest on her, almost inviting opposition, as if daring the staff to remind everyone who holds the strings here. Her fingers curl, nails biting into her palm beneath the table.

The nurses exchange glances. Emma Hayes, always steadfast but anxious today, shifts beside Lila, her teeth worrying her lower lip. Lila breathes in—the ozone tang of too-cold air, the waxy scent of floor polish. Too much silence. Too many resigned faces. Her chair slides back, loud against the linoleum.

"I'd like to say something." Her voice doesn't quaver. She pushes herself upright, standing clear in the glare of uneasy attention.

"Whatever is being suggested about how investigations are handled here, I haven't seen it reflected in my work with Dr. Hale. Last week—when an emergency landed in OR3—he was the only surgeon willing to stay past ten hours, double-checking every suture on a kid with a ruptured spleen. No shortcuts. No dismissals. Not a single action I would call 'privileged.' Maybe that's inconvenient for the rumors, but I call it doing the job."

There's a brief, sharp stillness. A breath, caught somewhere in the middle of the table.

A cluster of nurses exchange nervous whispers, but Lila holds her ground, her chin lifted. "Nobody here—no matter their rank—should be tried by gossip instead of facts. If we all start turning on each other just because someone outside these walls wants a scandal, who wins?"

Lila's words hang suspended in the antiseptic air, rippling outward. Across the table, Emma shoots her a glance—part anxiety, part pride.

A muffled cough, the creak of a chair. Dr. Crowe's jaw tightens. He folds his hands, his expression dark, but he doesn't interrupt. Victoria's lips thin. One board member—unknown to most staff—hunches her shoulders, scribbling something with a shaking hand.

"She's defending him? After what people have said?"

"You heard what happened in OR2..."

"There's always someone risking their neck for Hale."

Murmurs lap around Lila's ankles, threatening to pull her under, but she doesn't sit. She lets the current of discontent pass, even as her heartbeat thrums hard against her ribs. Crowe's eyes never leave her, narrowing, promising consequences. The weight of unspoken alliances swells inside the room; she sees who meets her gaze and who turns away.

Emma's voice, barely above a whisper, reaches her. "Lila's right. This isn't the place for witch hunts."

Those few words are enough to tip the room deeper into tension. Another nurse's eyes dart to the door, as if calculating escape. The board's notetaker—a senior woman with gray hair coiffed to perfection—makes a single, definite mark on her clipboard.

The fluorescent lights buzz and flicker. Papers shift. Conversations stall midair, the silence alive and bristling with the knowledge that nothing is settled, only paused. The meeting ends with no resolution, only the sound of nerves fraying and hope, stubborn, refusing to fall away.

Rain slants across the tall glass panels of the east wing as Darius moves down the corridor, his footsteps echoing between streaks of muted light and the hush of an emptied ward. The scent of ozone lingers—storm-washed, metallic, laced with the faint astringency of antiseptic that clings to this hospital no matter the hour. He stops by a wide hospital window, his jaw tight, the muscles in his neck fine-drawn beneath the collar of his coat. From this vantage point, the city outside smears into watercolors of gray and neon, untouchable behind glass. He welcomes the chill drafting in through a seam in the window frame. It numbs. It sharpens.

He doesn't watch for footsteps, but he feels them—the faint vibration, the subtle scrape of rubber soles. Lila appears at the far end, her silhouette taut with energy and a kind of aftershock stubbornness. Her hair is damp at the temples, her lips pressed together, her eyes alert to the invisible aftermath that clings to both of them. She halts a few paces away from him; neither speaks, the silence grown thick, stitched with remnants of accusation and defense that still reverberate back in the conference room.

Between them, the corridor hums. The elevator chimes in the distance; fluorescent bulbs flicker overhead, casting pale shadows against the walls. Somewhere, a code announcement mumbles through the intercom, too faint to decipher. The world out here feels suspended, a fragile truce cocooned in linoleum and glass.

Darius shifts. He faces her now, the lines around his mouth softening, though the intensity in his eyes does not waver. His hands, usually so still, close into fists and open again at his sides.

"You shouldn't have put yourself in their line of fire," he says quietly, his voice textured and low, barely carrying beyond her. For a heartbeat, his gaze flicks to the fluorescent glare, as if the light itself could dissipate the weight he carries. "It doesn't escape me... what that costs. Not here."

He doesn't know why the words feel so sharp in his mouth or why gratitude should ache. He has built his existence on boundaries—pristine, necessary, each one a scalpel-blade edge to keep pain at bay. And yet when Lila rose in that room, her voice steady, the margin between him and ruin felt suddenly less wide, less damning.

Lila draws in a quiet breath, letting it out slowly. She moves closer, enough that the rain's reflections ripple across both of their faces. There's a softness to her stance, but no retreat—an energy that says she has endured worse and will endure more if needed.

"I know exactly what it costs," she answers, her voice hushed but unwavering. "Maybe I should have stayed quiet. It would be simpler for both of us. But I won't stand by and watch them tear down a good doctor just because they think no one will question them." Her chin lifts, an echo of the defiance that rang through her words moments ago in the meeting. "I saw what you did for those patients, Darius. I'm not going to pretend otherwise, even if it means having to answer for it."

A beat. He studies her, searching for any flicker of uncertainty, but finds none. Heat blooms somewhere low in his chest—unfamiliar, coiling tight. The taste of rain ghosts across his lips; outside, thunder grumbles. The world narrows to the space between them and the current running underneath every word.

"I've spent years convincing myself I don't need anyone's defense," he murmurs, the admission rawer than any wound. "But today—" His voice catches. He isn't sure he has the language for this, isn't sure he even wishes to. "Thank you. For not walking away when it would have been easier."

She holds his gaze, her expression resolute. "You're not the only one with something to lose," she replies. "But there's more at stake here than our reputations. The truth deserves someone willing to fight for it—and some people"—her voice dips, laced with private meaning—"are worth the fallout."

Nothing in his training prepared him for this: the vulnerability of standing exposed with another soul, neither shielded nor alone. Darius registers, with sudden clarity, how isolation had grown around him like another organ, weighted and necessary. He has been unmoored since the scandal—existing behind glass, never letting anyone close enough to bruise him. Lila's defiance cracks something hidden, offering him a glimpse of another path.

He wonders—maybe too recklessly—if her courage might be the antidote he has refused for so long. What if he allowed himself to believe she could steady him, that solidarity might redress his failings where perfection never could? But darker currents tug: what if leaning on her makes her a target, folds his undoing around them both? The Brotherhood's games are never gentle. He is not built for hope, not after everything, yet hope ghosts in anyway.

They linger in the corridor, their silence turning fuller, weighted with the promise that neither is stepping back. He doesn't reach for her hand, but the space between them sizzles with all that isn't said.

At last, Darius steps away, his movements measured, almost brusque—a signal and a shield. Lila nods, her eyes steady, accepting the unspoken pact forged here. She turns in the opposite direction.

Their footsteps echo down the corridor, separate and unified, as the storm outside continues to drum its secret rhythm along the windows.

The Kiss in the Stairwell

The hallway is bright white and empty, with bare walls stretching on. Every step they take echoes as if the building itself is reacting. Darius walks beside Lila, both tired and weighed down as if they are wearing two sets of scrubs. At this time, the hospital feels less like a safe place and more like a confusing maze half-hidden in shadows. The usual busy sounds fade until only their quiet breathing and the hum of flickering old lights remain.

Ahead is a stairwell—forgotten and tucked between radiology and supply rooms. Its door is slightly ajar. Darius slows, lightly touching the metal door frame. The flickering light above makes his sharp face look like a ghostly shadow. He motions for Lila to come. She hesitates; the hallway behind them is empty. Together, they slip inside, the stairwell swallowing the usual hospital noise.

Cold concrete floors meet their feet. The air feels cool, with a faint smell of cleaning chemicals faded by time. A weak light above casts broken circles of light on Lila's face. Her hair is loose and messy, sweat and tiredness shining on her skin, the smell of menthol soap clinging to her like armor.

She crosses her arms, leans on the railing, and looks up at him—not to submit, but to challenge him.

"You're shutting me out, Darius," she says, holding back her voice but firm. "What are you afraid of?"

He stands with tense hands at his sides, his jaw tight. Many words swirl inside him. His first instinct is to push her away and keep quiet. But tonight, under the buzzing light and quiet concrete walls, something soft inside him struggles to breathe.

His eyes move away but then meet hers again. "I'm not afraid."

She steps closer, the space between them shrinking, the city and its demands disappearing outside the dirty window. Her voice softens. "You are. You don't have to tell me everything. I just need honesty, not perfection."

He exhales, thinking of all the times he hid—mistakes in surgery, the sharp pain of regret, the cold eyes of his bosses, and the Brotherhood's warnings. He used to think keeping distance was safer. What would it cost to let go, even for a moment?

Her hand brushes his sleeve, unsure. "Talk to me. Show me you can trust someone, even if it's just tonight."

His chest hurts. Something breaks—quiet and small. Before fear can take over, he steps closer. His hand lifts as if he might pull back, but instead, he cups her jaw, and their lips meet.

They kiss, and everything changes: footsteps on concrete, a slamming door far below, but none of it matters. Her lips taste salty-sweet, mixed with tired longing. He feels her heart beating unevenly under his touch. Her fingers grip his coat, grounding him more than he admits.

For a moment, everything between them disappears. Just this: lips searching, breath mixing, the silent yes to being alive together, breaking all the rules.

He pulls back quickly. The heat fades into cold. His eyes close briefly, caught between apology and desire. "I'm sorry," he whispers, his voice rough.

He steps back, removing himself, trying to rebuild the walls he put up. Guilt flashes on his face, stronger than anything she could say. In his mind, he pictures hospital staff coming down the stairs, the lights revealing them, whispered rumors reaching the Brotherhood. Every beat of longing is a risk, a threat, a betrayal.

He leaves, his steps echoing down the stairs—fast and unsteady—swallowed by darkness.

Lila stands in the dim light, her hand near her lips where his warmth lingered. The stairwell is very quiet now. Secret tension fills the air between metal railings and worn walls; only distant water drops and a vent can be heard.

Uncertainty fills her. The feeling between them hasn't faded—if anything, being apart has made it sharper. She wonders if the building itself will remember this moment—the place where boundaries broke, where desire was stronger than fear, and where one forbidden kiss could change everything.

She stays there, caught between past and hope. The hallway beyond is cold and empty—but for now, she stays, hands shaking, heart beating with the promise and danger of what just started.

Darius Hale's office glows with a dull, yellowed light. The clock ticks loudly, each tick pressing on his mind. His computer screen glows green with blurred medical records. His raw hands press to his temples.

He listens to the silence—the empty hospital, clean and cold, hiding the evidence of pain.

His mind won't calm down. It locks on memories. Caius Drake's big figure sitting in a leather chair, warning him—"You're never alone, Hale. Remember the code." Lucien Blackwell's cold eyes and words: "Power comes from silence and sacrifice. Anything else is weakness." The Brotherhood's voices echo in his chest—loyalty, secrecy, control. Their rules wrap tightly around his life, choking any hope of stepping away. He imagines Caius's eyes if he told him how he feels now. Disappointment, hard loyalty, a cold chill.

But beneath all this, his fingers remember the skin that held his. Lila's hand, warm from a patient's pulse, over his in the stairwell. Lila standing close, breaking through the mask he has worn since losing someone in surgery. Her lips—a wild promise touching his—taste of courage and sweetness. His throat tightens with what he might lose.

He knows he already failed the Brotherhood once—one mistake in surgery, one doubt, an error that haunts his nights. Headlines show how regret can destroy. He rebuilt himself with hard work and silence. He is the perfect surgeon who never slips. He can't carry doubt or feelings.

Still, here it is—living in the dark office like a sickness. What if he can't remove it?

He imagines worst-case scenarios. Someone whispering Lila's name, an orderly pausing too long, rumors spreading through nursing stations, reaching the boardroom and Brotherhood leaders. Does Victoria Grant notice Lila's late breaks? Does Crowe watch her too closely? Every tick brings the chance of being found out.

If someone really sees them—really knows—what then? Scandal at the hospital. The Brotherhood will act quickly and harshly to cut out any weak links. Lila could lose her job, her dignity, and become a warning for others. He imagines her family targeted next, their lives ruined by forces too powerful.

Worse, the Brotherhood cannot be stopped by asking or shame. Their history is full of broken rebels. His loyalty is a deep, painful scar. His vows carry weight that won't let him ignore them—even now, with clenched fists, pain in his head, and desire choking him. He is afraid. Not of exile, but of causing pain others have suffered before.

The clock ticks on. His eyes rest on a dusty photo above the cabinet—a surgical team under bright lights, their clothes stained, hands linked after a win. This was where he believed redemption was—in healing. This photo was the last thing his mother praised, the only family relic left.

He wonders if true redemption is saving lives or fiercely protecting the people you love. He touches the cold photo frame, real under his fingers.

A knock at the door: what would Caius say? That feeling love for a nurse endangers all? He runs through Brotherhood rules—sharp and harsh, pushing for his isolation.

But something inside him shifts—a steady feeling under his ribs. He won't let her become a victim. He won't hide love away with unfinished work and cold files. For the first time since the loss, he considers defending desire—not out of guilt, but out of strength. A hope begins in his chest. Fragile, but there.

He closes the patient file and turns off the lamp. Darkness swallows the room—thick and unjudging. He sits with it, heart pounding, holding on to the image of Lila like a secret fire that won't die. He knows, no matter the rules, this longing won't let go.

The break room is a small space in the big hospital, with an old vending machine humming beside a chipped green door. Lila sits curled up on a worn couch, her knees tight to her chest, arms wrapped around herself. The fabric is dusty with crumbs and years of secrets—quiet talks, tired laughter stolen between emergencies. Tonight, silence hangs heavy over the hospital, broken only by flickering harsh lights.

She touches her lips lightly, searching for any warmth left from Darius's kiss. The memory floods her—a moment frozen in the cold stairwell: his shaking hand, quick breath, lips pressing against hers with pain and need. Her heart still races, caught there in that quiet, beneath the flickering stairwell light.

Did she imagine it? Or did something real spark in that silence? Darius Hale, so perfect and cold, letting his walls fall for just one moment—was she just looking for meaning where there was only regret? It feels like the world is holding its breath, waiting on the soft power of a stolen kiss.

"You still here?" Emma's voice cuts in from the hall. She leans on the door, half-lit by the flickering light. "You look like someone told you the world's ending at 3 a.m."

Lila forces a smile that doesn't reach her eyes. "Maybe it is," she says softly.

Emma plops down on the coffee table edge, elbows on her knees. "Whatever's bothering you, it's not worth it. Except if it's about Crowe finally tripping over himself and hitting a trauma cart. Then I want to hear about it."

Lila laughs quietly, rough and tired. Emma is warm—a reminder of normalcy in this tough place where people get hard to survive. "Not that. Just... a rough shift," she says.

Emma looks at her, skeptical, then gives in. "If you want out, I'll clock you early and make up a reason. No one checks HR forms anyway."

"I'll stay," Lila says more strongly than she means. "I'm fine."

Emma raises an eyebrow but stands and ruffles Lila's hair gently, like scolding a child. "Your call, chica. But if you need help, whistle." She leaves, the door closing softly behind her.

The room is quiet again. The hospital shrinks back to flickering light and the stale smell of old coffee. Fear creeps in as she turns the stairwell kiss over and over in her mind like a smooth stone—what does this mean? Her muscles ache from hours of standing, and under her scrubs, her skin tingles with cold and doubt. Loving Darius isn't just foolish—it's dangerous. Hospital rumors are sharp, alive, and the Brotherhood's shadow covers every hall. One word or careless moment could ruin everything: her job, her family, the small hope she gathers each shift.

Pictures crowd her mind—angry bosses, the wrong nurse seen at the wrong time, doors left open. She sees her family's faces too: Mateo, stubborn and hurting beyond his years. Losing this job, even for a short time, would push them into darkness she's fought to escape. One mistake, and they'd all suffer for her choices.

She hides her face in her hands, rough from the sanitizer and work, breathing shallow as anxiety grips her chest. But beneath the fear, something shines—memories not of Darius as an untouchable figure, but as a man breaking in her arms, letting fear and longing shake him. She recalls the tremble in his fingers, the soft surrender in his voice when he whispered her name. Real. Vulnerable.

She's survived a lot—nights holding Mateo when nightmares woke him, doctors who act like nurses are servants, silent fights against despair on endless shifts. She's seen how fragile people break, how rumors can hurt, and how power is always in someone's hand. And she has survived.

She stands and walks to the window. The city outside shines under rain and distant thunder, a storm coming, chaos near. Her face reflects faintly in the dark glass, her eyes new—stronger, marked with determination.

She turns away, her jaw tight. She won't let Darius hide behind his cold walls, not after tonight, not after seeing the man beneath the guilt and control. If loving him is dangerous, she'll face it. If the Brotherhood moves against them, if the hospital turns cold, she will stand.

"I will fight for you," she says quietly, unsure if it's a promise to Darius, the world, or herself. The storm outside grows louder—the future breaking open with lightning.

Shoulders back, Lila leaves the worn couch and steps into the dark hallway, calm and brave at last, the night holding its secrets as thunder rolls far away.

Hospital Politics

Midday light shines through strong glass, casting faint lines on the conference table. The air in the boardroom feels heavy with tension. Every movement is sharp, and every whisper is planned. Outside the thick glass walls, the hospital's steady noise—the intercom beeps, footsteps, and the clinking of coffee spoons—is faint. Inside, the room feels fragile as board members arrive.

Soft murmurs follow them—the sound of fancy jackets brushing against clean white coats, and nervous fingers holding gold pens. Dr. Sebastian Crowe sits at the end of the table, calm but alert, one leg crossed. A woman sits by a plaque honoring the biggest donor; a man with a rival hospital's emblem on his jacket keeps his phone face down, ready to react.

Victoria Grant stands, moving with careful grace: her shoulders shift slightly, and her heels click softly on the polished floor. She picks up the remote, and the screens light up—a cool blue glow spreads over the table. Reports, bank records, and surgery logs appear as rows of numbers, red marks, and digital signatures. The projector hums quietly.

"Let's start," Victoria says, her voice calm but firm. She ignores the noise of the electronics, quiet whispers, and the sharp, clean smell mixed with a hint of expensive cologne. She stands strong. She reads each accusation clearly: missing medicine records, patient results under review, and secret emails hinting at wrongdoing.

Underneath her calm voice, there is fear and caution. She knows the room is filled with distrust—alliances made with a look, cracks forming between former friends. The Brotherhood has always worked behind the hospital's clean surface, influencing donations and private clinics. Now, opponents challenge them openly, using ethics and public trust as a cover, but driven by old grudges and power plays.

Victoria feels old pain under her skin. She remembers how a rumor or a lost file could end a career here. There is no room for mistakes in this glass room.

As the evidence is shown, a board member leans forward. The donor plaque reflects in her glasses. Another board member, whose family name is the subject of gossip, twists a silver ring and narrows his eyes. Information flows—facts and guesses. Each word cuts deep. Victoria's hands stay steady, but inside, her heart pounds—a warning of what is at risk.

"Someone has been thorough," Dr. Crowe says quietly, breaking the silence with dark meaning. "There is a pattern of problems. Strange that every chart involved links to the same department, sometimes even—the same people." He moves his finger along the digital timeline. "Notes unsigned. Secret testimony. We are being watched as much as we watch others."

A woman nearby scoffs, watching the screens with a hard look. "Or someone is making a false trail to fit their goals. We all know what threats can do here. Today it's Dr. Hale. Tomorrow, maybe anyone here?"

Crowe's eyes cool. "If the hospital's name falls under scandal, no one is safe." His words hang heavy like the smell of machine oil on gloves.

Another man murmurs about politics, his voice shaking with anger. "This is classic. Power struggles, old money saving failing places. Now the Brotherhood wants the whole hospital, not just the old parts."

"That's enough," a voice shouts, but it is lost as gavels tap and people shout for order. Victoria grips the table, watching anger rise and the group split into fights.

"We have rules—" a man starts.

"Rules don't matter if the board is corrupt—"

"The real problem is the outside influence you bring—"

"Be careful what you say—"

Noise explodes, voices raised, the gavel lost in chaos. Victoria's eyes move to the screens, then to every face—calculating who is a threat, who can be trusted, and what pain or gains will come from this fight.

Voices clash sharply.

"You protect your friends—don't pretend otherwise!"

"I protect the hospital's honesty. You bring grudges and expect us to fall?"

"Grudges? This is about facts—facts you soften because he's useful to you."

"My group? At least we don't take bribes from outsiders like some here."

Victoria finally stands tall, her voice cutting through the noise. "Enough." The room falls silent, the sound echoing against the glass. Her jaw is tight, her eyes hard.

"This meeting is over. Until the evidence is fully checked, no more talks." She moves from the bright table, her face shadowed and unreadable, and leaves the room.

The board members stay seated, watching each other as new tensions settle quietly everywhere.

In a nearly empty hospital hallway, where fluorescent lights fade into evening quiet, Darius walks carefully. The noise of carts and nurses' voices fades behind him as he nears a door with a small, plain brass number. Inside, Lucien Blackwell waits, standing in a way that sends a clear signal: sit down.

The office is small and without windows, lit only by sunbeams cutting across the wall through blinds. Dust floats in the warm air, disturbed each time a door nearby closes.

"Darius. Sit," Lucien says quickly, serious. His hands are folded on the desk, steady and precise.

The silence here feels heavier than elsewhere in the hospital; the air smells of old leather and overheated wiring. Darius sits on a worn chair, cooled by air conditioning fighting summer heat.

"There's no time to play games," Lucien says, tapping his fingers once. Papers lie straight in front of him. "The board is moving faster than we thought. This is about you and more. You know that?"

Darius watches the light stripes moving on Lucien's cuff, his own reflection faint in the desk glass. His chest tightens. He's felt the fear all day—hallway whispers, looks turned away, even from those who once respected him. It's a familiar pain, but months away have made him less sure. Here with Lucien, the stakes feel real and raw.

"They want a quick punishment," Lucien says slowly, choosing words carefully. "To calm the public and warn others. This isn't about just names. It's about the Brotherhood's power—what we control outside the hospital. That could disappear overnight."

A heavy quiet fills the room. Darius presses his hands on his pants, trying to stay calm.

Lucien slides a folder to him. The seal is unbroken—a sign of trust, or maybe a test. "Look at this. Messages linking Grant, Mason, and some suppliers. Not open talks, but patterns. Watch for points where outside vendors connect—especially those known to be linked."

The folder lands softly. Darius doesn't open it yet. His throat feels dry, like old metal. The Brotherhood's rule: trust only what you can prove. He's learned to keep himself inside invisible walls—cold and controlled—but every new accusation cracks his foundation a little more. Lucien watches him closely, looking for weakness.

"You must act like everything you say publicly is recorded. Every unsanctioned meeting, nod, or handshake can be twisted. Understand?"

Darius nods, though the words twist inside. Despite his training, some wounds won't heal. He thinks of Lila—her hopeful eyes, tired but strong voice. He won't let this rot touch her. But here, betrayal is as common as scrubbed floors, worn by friends and helpers alike.

Lucien leans forward. Light stripes shine through his gray hair. "We think Crowe's anger isn't just rivalry. They're stirring fights. Someone is feeding rumors and records, trying to start a war. Our enemies wait for the Brotherhood to break, for someone to slip."

A chill runs down Darius's neck. His hands clench the folder in his lap, knuckles tapping it once. This is what they don't say out loud: if the Brotherhood falls, the city's hospitals become prey. Safety nets will fail—patients and staff left to whoever pays the most. In the end, no one is safe—not even him or those he loves—not even the walls he's built.

He wonders briefly how trust becomes betrayal. He imagines the Brotherhood headquarters dark, files burning in hidden places—Lila's name crossed out in lists. His fate sealed not by enemies, but by those sworn to protect him. If he slips, every step pulls another thread loose.

Lucien's gaze stays fixed. "Now, loyalty must be proven, not assumed. Especially now."

Darius stands, chair scraping linoleum. He nods once, straightening his back. The folder feels cold in his hand as he leaves, shadows following. He walks away, jaw firm, breath steady but heart beating unevenly. The battle has changed. Silence is no longer safe.

At St. Gabriel's, afternoon turns to evening, mixing the hospital's sharp, clean smell with the soft scent of rain outside. In back offices and VIP lounges, quiet urgent talks swirl over the usual hospital noise—a different kind of rhythm. Light reflects off shiny tabletops onto anxious hands, security badges, and papers left unopened.

In a small executive room, Sebastian Crowe leans over a table set with clean carafes and untouched pastries. His stiff cuff brushes a manila folder filled with names and times printed out. An administrator with a diamond tie slides a gray envelope toward him, quiet as a trick. Their words barely rise above the ventilation hum: "If they need a scapegoat, let's not make it one of ours. The board listens—if promises are kept." Sebastian's smirk is quick, never revealing his full thoughts.

Nearby, another group occupies a private lounge usually reserved for investors. Here, bright lights erase emotion from a supervisor's face as she receives a note—no name, just a threat hidden in hospital terms: "Loyalty is a balance sheet. Owe the wrong side, pay the price." Her fingers grip the page. Her voice shakes barely as she makes a call, eyes darting to the door as if she could spot Lila Moreno herself, whose career now hangs by a thread.

In the halls, gossip spreads like infection underneath the alarms' hum. Encrypted messages pop on screens under lab coats, short and urgent: "Purge soon. Darius's team first?" "Saw him with Blackwell. Something's breaking." Rumors fly between nurses at vending machines, traveling like cold wind. Names whispered in corners—Darius, Lila, even Emma. The warmth once shared during holiday shifts has turned into careful formality and sideways looks. Where hands once gave comfort, now there is silence, hands hover over files before pulling back.

Darius feels the cold in every step along St. Gabriel's halls. Around him are reminders of a world he led—donor photos, plaques with the Orion symbol, shiny floors under his steady walk. Colleagues turn away as he passes, conversations stopping mid-sentence. A young resident he helped last year points just above Darius's shoulder and hurries off, tablet held like armor. A surgical nurse, who shared a quiet laugh with him days ago, offers only a quick nod, cheeks flushing red.

Only Emma Hayes, outside Radiology with arms crossed, dares a real look. Her eyes flick to Lila as she passes—worry clear, lips tight—before she joins a group heading to the elevators. Even loyalty is under strain, threatened by the machines turning behind closed doors.

Darius's mind churns between steps and looks. Every slight, every short greeting or avoided eye, presses on memories heavy with guilt—a memory of blood on gloves, silence after a monitor flatlined, blame that won't fade. Allies he trusted—Caius, Lucien, the Brotherhood's leaders—have become distant watchers, their support withered by doubt. Old trust breaks faster than bone under pressure.

This hurt is deeper, fresh every time he sees silence follow him, how talks resume only after he's gone. It's quiet betrayal, slowly eating away, deeper than public blame: even the loyal bend in fear. The need to regain control—over the story, over fate—is a steady beat beneath his calm, a challenge hardwired in him. But the city outside and the Brotherhood inside have both grown colder. Even Lila, strong and defiant, approaches more cautiously—her looks both anchor and warning.

In a dim office, a tense conversation breaks:

"They're coming for him—you know it too," a board member says quietly.

"And if they win? Who's next? We all have blood on our hands."

"That's why no one is safe unless they choose sides."

In a cramped lounge, urgency sharpens words:

"If you think siding with Crowe keeps you safe, you're wrong," a nurse whispers.

"I'm not here to be safe," another replies, smiling fiercely. "I'm here to keep my job."

Afternoon fades, the hospital's ordered mask slips. Darius slows near a big window, the city pale and wet beyond the glass. Reflected in the glass is Sebastian Crowe's smile—quick and cruel. Darius's hand tightens on the sill. He closes his eyes. Behind him, alliances shift and break in real time, every secret smile a reminder: You are alone.

The halls grow quiet. Darius, tall and alone, watches the dark swallow the city, his reflection now haunted by enemies.

The auditorium glows under rows of lights, casting patterns over a sea of suits, uniforms, and nervous faces. The air smells of wet concrete and perfume, damp air coming in through the revolving doors. Quiet and tense, the crowd buzzes with held-back energy. On stage, microphones shine, and at the podium stands Victoria Grant—a calm figure in navy silk—her eyes measuring everyone.

Outside, thunder rumbles against worn glass. Each boom shakes the rows, making shoulders tense. Phone cameras click quietly, and notepads rustle softly before the event, while overhead lights flicker and hum.

Victoria begins, her voice steady. "Because of recent findings, the St. Gabriel's board must open a public inquiry into Dr. Darius Hale's work and ethics." She clicks the remote; blue light shows charts and emails on the screen. Her words are sharp and clear, like a careful cut, but beneath the surface, there is steel.

People near the front shift. Some cough quietly, while others look down, fidgeting with rings or labels on water bottles. A wave passes through the hall like the swell before a big wave. Whispers move among journalists, doctors, and board members—each look heavy with rumors and hidden hopes.

From the third row, Dr. Sebastian Crowe stands, perfect in a dark suit. His voice is low and strong.

"We must face hard facts. Anonymous staff gave detailed records—surgeries changed without explanation, patients sent through VIP areas, strange prescription logs." Crowe moves, hands behind his back, scanning for support. "Saint Gabriel's can't be a place for secret groups or deals." His words linger, like salt on a wound. Gasps ripple. Eyes shift between Darius, Victoria, and the screen full of proof.

Victoria's jaw tightens, but she stays silent. A nervous laugh breaks the quiet from the back. A pair of board members share a secret look in the aisle. One points at a small Brotherhood pin on her lapel. Another's face hardens—the political undercurrents show even in tight breath and stiff posture.

Lightning flashes bright and fast, lighting up the tense faces. Darius stands near the aisle, arms crossed tight. His gaze sweeps the room: administrators whispering secretly, worried surgical staff leaning forward. He spots Lila in the back, her lips pressed, brows furrowed—holding herself steady like she's fighting a storm alone. Seeing her under these lights, brave but afraid, stirs something sharp and soft inside him.

Among the sound of pens and quiet murmurs, Lucien Blackwell appears near the heavy doors. He moves calm and steady, like always. When Darius steps toward the exit—pulled by pressure or desperation—Lucien places a hand on his arm, stopping him before the shadows.

"Don't give them your anger, Darius. Stay strong. Friends fall away when trapped—sometimes even family." His words are low but cut deep. "Tonight is not just about truth. It's about surviving. Watch out for attacks from inside."

Darius's muscles tense, his skin buzzing with tension. He looks at Lucien's calm reflection in the glass, then back to the crowd, searching for surety in the chaos.

"Why now?" he whispers. "Why push so hard, all at once?"

Lucien's answer is a sad smile. "Because now, you're weak. And because someone promised them everything if you fall."

A camera flash pops nearby; sweat beads on Darius's brow. The hall feels like a test, every eye waiting for him to break.

Reporters shout questions. "Dr. Hale—did you fake records?" "Is the Brotherhood blackmailing staff?" "Did you trade favors for patient referrals?" Each hits him like cold rain. He tries to keep calm, but his heart pounds hard. The truth, what he always trusted, now feels fragile as glass.

He meets Lila's eyes. Her hand shakes as she holds a chair, her jaw tight with fierce hope. For a moment, he imagines the storm outside taking her away from this harsh light—but he knows she will stand strong, no matter what comes.

Every breath tastes like thunder and doubt. If he fails, the Brotherhood will split. His career and reputation will burn. Lila's future will be caught in the wreckage of his past. This inquiry isn't the end—it's the start of a long battle. Behind the accusations, old ties break, the Brotherhood tested by fire and betrayal. Loyalty is no longer a shield but a secret question whispered in dark corners.

As thunder pounds and rain pours, Darius lifts his chin. He clenches his fists until his knuckles turn white, holding on to the only promise he's kept: protect Lila, even if everything else burns. Lightning strikes, and the lights flicker out. For a moment, no one breathes. The war isn't over—it has only just begun.

Betrayal in White Coats

A hush clings to the velvet shadows of the lounge, barely disturbed by the jazz that floats from a hidden corner speaker—low, throaty, conspiratorial. The financial district outside thrums with neon veins, but here, the light hesitates. A single bulb glows dimly over each booth, their tables lacquered to a mirror finish, scenes of private rendezvous ghosting across the surface.

Dr. Sebastian Crowe slips in through the alley entrance. The door bears no sign—just brushed steel marked by a faint codepad smudge, the scent of cigarette smoke lingering at the threshold. It is not a place for the curious. The air inside is dense with the sting of gin and expensive perfume, the faint citrus twist in every exhale. He pauses, scanning for faces. No one greets him; regulars know never to acknowledge a new arrival.

He moves with purpose, his suit jacket perfectly fitted, shoes silent on the thick carpet, until he spots the secluded booth veiled behind latticework screens. Victoria Grant waits—elegance incarnate in a midnight suit, her eyes sharp and cold beneath the fragile halo of a chandelier. The second figure is three-quarters in shadow, a silhouette defined by a platinum cufflink and a profile sculpted by old power.

They don't stand to greet him. Their body language is all calculation: fingers drumming softly, posture guarded but unafraid. Crowe eases down across from them, folding his hands. The table's chill seeps into his palms—a silent reminder of what's at stake.

For all of St. Gabriel's dazzling corridors and whispered piety, its pulse is kept by men and women who trust secrets more than scalpel or oath. Loyalty is currency, sharpened by favors, bartered in locked rooms. Deals are struck in clinics, on midnight stairwells, and over encrypted calls routed through distant servers. And sometimes, at a table like this. The real surgeons of power cut reputations, not flesh.

Tonight, the stakes are clinical and cold: altered records, misplaced blame, the slow rot of trust. A career can be ended with a single keystroke, a reputation hollowed by rumors spun from digital smoke. Those who master these shadows never sleep easy, for the walls are thin, and every triumph carries a taste of blood.

Victoria leans in, a hint of gin lingering on her breath, and slides a slim flash drive across the table. The metal winks in the low light, the logo barely visible. Crowe's lips twitch—satisfaction, maybe, or perhaps nerves.

The other adversary pushes forward a file of documents, hospital watermarks blurred by a careless hand. Names and dates—so many altered, so many meant to wound. A faint scent of paper and printer ink mingles with the room's cologne as Crowe flips through, his jaw clenched.

"It's all here," Victoria says, her voice glacial. "The upload protocol is built in. Three p.m.—after shift change, before the weekly audit."

"And the alert?" Crowe's voice is smooth, but behind every word, there's impatience, a hunger for the next move.

"A tip-off—anonymous, timed from inside." The man in the shadows speaks softly. "Leadership can't ignore it. Once it hits, neither can Hale."

He slides the papers back. Their eyes lock—hers calculating, his unreadable. Trust is an illusion in this business, but for now, their interests align.

"The envelope," Victoria says quietly, as if it's the password. He nods.

A heavy, cream-colored envelope crosses the table, its seal embossed. Crowe feels the weight—cash thinly disguised as legal fees, more than enough incentive for a reputation at risk. His fingers linger on it. He finds he wants to appear casual in front of these sharks, but his heart races in his chest.

They rise—no farewells, no empty promises—just a quiet, orchestrated shuffle as they slip away through separate exits. Crowe lingers last, cradling the flash drive, the cool plastic digging into his palm. The lounge's low light glances off the windshield of a black car idling at the curb beyond the frosted glass. For a moment, his face is a fractured reflection—hazel eyes, the scar at his brow sharp, features warped and multiplied in glossy black. He studies the lines, searching for certainty and finding only intensity, the edges of himself threatening to come undone.

Beneath all the polish of the city and the hospital, a war rages deeper than most will ever sense. The Brotherhood rules through influence and favor, but there is always an undercurrent—rivals hungry for a taste of control, outcasts willing to torch reputations for a seat at the table. Private pacts decide the fate of the brilliant and the damned;

mastery is not just skill in the OR, but the ability to thrive in these currents—saboteur and survivor all at once.

He imagines Darius—the untouchable, the golden favorite—brought low by a torrent of perfectly timed accusations. Part of Crowe is giddy at the thought, but another part wonders: How many lines has he already crossed for this? His future is balanced here, between their greed and his own shadowed ambition, the risk of exposure sharpening every plan.

With the lingering taste of gin on his tongue, Sebastian makes a vow to the city beyond the glass and to the storm gathering in his chest. Darius Hale will fall. Tonight is just the first incision.

Inside the luminous heart of St. Gabriel's Hospital, a server hums softly behind the boardroom's glass walls. Atop a teak desk, a cluster of senior administrators huddle over a monitor, their faces caught in sharp slices of LED light. The afternoon's pulse pounds through the hospital—the echo of rolling carts, the sharp clatter of code alarms, the antiseptic tang in the air. But now, a different current runs beneath: one of suspicion, raw and electric.

A secretary, her eyes rimmed red from too much screen time, double-checks a fresh batch of notifications. Her fingertip hovers over the trackpad as lines of text flicker: incident reports, unsigned PDF scans, and error logins, all implicating Darius Hale with clinical, remorseless detail. Complications in surgery. Discrepancies in anesthetic orders. Each file is a whispered accusation rendered brutally permanent. She exhales in a tight sob, glancing at the rows of names—most she recognizes, but the weight of altered dates and new admissions pulls her mouth into a grim line.

Just outside the glass, Dr. Sebastian Crowe glides through the nurse's station, his gaze narrowed and self-satisfied beneath the cruel fluorescence. He joins a cluster of surgeons, his voice tucked into the hush of uncertainty.

"Unbelievable, isn't it?" Crowe murmurs as two colleagues lean in, drawn by the promise of revelation and concealed judgment. "Have you heard what's been circulating about Hale?" His lips barely move, yet the words travel, poisonous and slow as a spilled sedative.

A senior anesthesiologist, cheeks blanched to sallow, tugs a fellow aside by the elbow. His whisper is hoarse, cracked by nerves. "They can't be real. Darius—he's not careless." His companion's lips pinch white. "Maybe not, but the files... they're stacked deep. If the board's seen them, it won't matter." Both men cast covert glances toward Darius's darkened office down the hall, uneasy shadows collecting between their words.

Down in the ER, Lila Moreno pushes through a thicket of noise and commotion. Cold rushes of air trail in her wake as she weaves past trauma bays, the copper-bright scent of blood clinging to her gloves. She feels the shift starting before she sees it—a hush trailing her, the subtle veer of bodies. An orderly who'd once swapped jokes with her won't meet her eyes. He stares intently at his clipboard, pen tapping out some frantic Morse. A lab tech, a wiry man with kind eyes, suddenly ducks behind a battery cart, whispering harshly to two nurses huddled beside the medication fridge.

Their voices filter through: "That was definitely Hale's patient." "But someone said he wasn't even on shift." "Doesn't matter—everyone's talking about it." The trio glances furtively at the chart snagged in Lila's grasp—Darius's name at the top in crisp ink. Color prickles under Lila's skin. She tightens her grip, her knuckles whitening, and strides on as if weightless, determined not to crumple under the growing suspicion that coats every gesture, every breath.

Emma Hayes is waiting at the end of the next corridor, her eyes scanning the chaos for a safe moment. She grabs Lila's wrist, pulling her into an equipment closet that smells of bleach, latex, and everything hidden. The sudden dark, cool shelter muffles their words. Emma keeps her voice low, her eyes darting to the crack beneath the door.

"I overheard two residents—third floor, just now," Emma says, her breath shaky but fierce. "They're talking about refusing to scrub in if Darius leads. They argue he's a liability. One said the board's already looking for a replacement." She sags back against the metal shelves, her fists tightening.

"They don't know anything," Lila whispers, her voice scraped thin by both hope and exhaustion. "This isn't him. Someone wants him out, and right now, we're letting them divide us."

"That's the problem. They're scared. Even people who used to defend him—they're starting to doubt. You have to see that, Lila." Emma's hand trembles at her side. "If someone's pushing this—inside the hospital—it'll get worse. We don't know who we can trust. Not anymore."

"I'll talk to him. He deserves to know the truth." Lila's chest aches—not just for Darius but for the silent destruction unraveling friendships in these walls. "We can't just abandon him—to rumors, to lies."

Emma's mouth twists, uncertainty shadowing her confidence. "What if there's more? What if helping him... what if it makes us targets, too?"

Lila glances away, tracing the outline of the closet handle. "Then we stand together. Even if the ground's moving under us."

The closet presses close—a kingdom of supplies, of secrets—and for a heartbeat, the only sound is Emma's uneven breathing and the distant, rhythmic beep of a monitor outside.

The door opens, and light spills in. Lila steps out first, blinking in the flood of sterile brilliance and urgent activity. The corridor's hum washes back: announcements overhead, the clatter of gurneys, voices now sharp with trepidation. She feels the shift more keenly—the way glances slide off her, the way a tech freezes mid-sentence, feigning absorption in paperwork.

Trust had always been the fragile glue holding this place together. Now it hangs threadbare—dispersed by a few digital accusations and the right whispers at the right time, expertly poisoned. Lila's thoughts swirl: who started it, who benefits, whether she herself stands out too much when she defends him. She's not sure if conviction will be enough, but she can't let fear decide who she is. There's too much at stake—for Darius, for everyone whose hands keep this hospital running, for herself.

Her phone vibrates, sharp and insistent against her thigh. There it is—a hospital-wide alert crawling across the screen: Dr. Darius Hale—please report to boardroom two, immediately. Lila's heart lodges in her throat. For a moment, everything else is lost—the wariness, the noise, the alliances burned in secret shadow. Only the sense that battles can begin and end here, in a corridor, heartbeat by heartbeat, as rain smudges the glass and thunder rolls, distant and approaching.

The silence in Darius Hale's office is thick, pressed beneath the faint hiss of the central air and the metallic scent of disinfectant clinging to polished glass. The world outside the window bruises into indigo, city lights casting their fractured glow in rows upon the reflective floor.

Evening is in its closing grip. Here, all is precise—no errant files on the desk, no evidence of fatigue except for the shifting shadow beneath his high-backed chair. He is reaching for a pen when something soft brushes against his office door, barely audible. He waits, resisting the urge to move too quickly, then stands and moves with that familiar controlled grace, his footsteps muffled by carpet.

A folded white envelope lies at the threshold, crisp and anonymous. He stoops, noting the lack of distinguishing fingerprints or insignia, and flips it open, the paper whispering between his fingers. "You cannot win—leave now or lose everything." The words are stark, black, and impersonal. He runs his thumb along the edge, as if the pressure could reveal who sent it. For a moment, his jaw tightens, muscle jumping beneath his skin, and his eyes flicker—just for a heartbeat—with something almost vulnerable.

The message lingers in his grip as he turns toward his desk. He logs in to his computer, his fingertips drumming on the keyboard. Each key click is sharper than usual. The familiar hospital admin screen flashes—then stalls, loading longer than it ever has. Several file folders are grayed out, padlocked. Darius narrows his eyes. He bypasses protocols, inputs a series of credentials known only to attending surgeons. Still, the records refuse him, as if the institution itself is conspiring.

Navigating to the surgical reports for last week's emergency aortic repair, he uncovers notes appended in his name—entries citing improper technique, delayed response, and critical lapses he knows to be fiction. Their phrasing mimics his own, calculated and detached, but the clinical precision is off, emotions injected into what should be cold fact. He scrolls to another case. The outcome is revised, a clean recovery transformed with a keystroke into a complication. It is a ghostly rewriting, a trap laid with the intellect of someone inside the walls. Cold sweat beads along his spine.

A memory surfaces: ten months ago, a tragedy of blood and shrieking monitors, the night he lost a patient he believed he could save. The surgical suite had been so bright it burned, and after, there was nothing but the Brotherhood's silence and shame. The ghost of that night has followed every step since—the surgical gloves he can never quite take off, the light he can never soften.

Darius snaps the laptop shut, steeling himself. He leaves the message on his desk as if expecting it to multiply while he is gone. The hospital corridor outside his office is lit with an artificial sky-blue, the distant clangor of gurneys carried through the sterile air. He walks with none of the hesitance he feels, purposeful, untouchable in his black suit.

Outside the boardroom, a knot of executives cluster, their voices low, body language closed like fistfuls of secrets. As his figure approaches, their words choke into silence. One woman, pin-thin and with a surgeon's practiced composure, glances at him with quick calculation—then looks away. The group disperses hastily, the drag of expensive shoes on tile the only tribute to their presence. Darius keeps walking, his expression unreadable, but the isolation bites.

Past the turn, near the operating rooms, the lights sharpen—the world narrows to glistening steel and antiseptic. Here, waiting, Dr. Sebastian Crowe leans against the marbled wall, arms crossed, a smile heartbreakingly smug.

"Darius. Still standing," Crowe murmurs, his voice like velvet over a scalpel. "You do seem to survive an impressive number of catastrophes." He steps forward, his eyes hooded. "You know, sometimes mistakes linger longer than genius. Ghosts, if you will. Even the greats can fall, and it's rarely graceful."

Darius's gaze is ice. "Enjoying yourself, Sebastian? You think this passes for subtlety?" The words are quiet, dispassionate, but fury veins beneath. "This has your stink all over it. But you never did have the stomach to act alone. Who's helping you? Whose leash are you on?"

Crowe's mouth lifts at one corner—a lion relishing a wounded rival. "Not everything is about you, Hale. Power shifts. Sometimes the old gods have to die to make way for the new. Some men are overdue for a fall." He shrugs, pushing off the wall, and his shoes are near-silent as he disappears down the corridor.

For a moment, Darius stands alone, haloed in clinical glare, the faint reek of burnt coffee and stress from the nurses' station reaching him. He presses his palm against cool tile, his eyes briefly closed. Anger warps into something sharper—resolve, painful and clear. He can retreat. Give in to the pull of shame and memory, let the Brotherhood close ranks without him. But he doesn't move. In his chest, something steadies, battered but unbroken. No adversary—secret or brazen—will force him to abandon his vows or Lila. His fear is an old scar. He survived the first rupture. He'll endure this.

Darius straightens, his jaw set, his eyes cold and clear. He pivots and strides back toward his office, his heart pounding with the certainty that the battle is just beginning. With every step, he tightens his grip on control, cataloging each fragile piece of evidence, preparing for war.

The Choice to Stay

Lila unlocks the door quietly, the rain outside making a soft sound. She steps into the warm apartment and closes the door with her hip. The air smells faintly of reheated beans and burnt cinnamon toast from earlier. She drops her hospital bag onto the worn carpet near the door. Her old, pale blue Nikes scrape against the fabric as she moves inside, a reminder of her usual routine.

The hallway light flickers over the small living room. The kitchen table is covered with unpaid bills, urgent notices stamped in red, grocery lists, and prescription papers. A used candle sits atop a pile of electricity bills. The rain taps against the window, matching the quick beat of Lila's heart.

Mateo sits on the couch with a math workbook in his hands, frowning as he silently reads and tries to remember formulas. Their younger sister lies wrapped in a patchwork blanket on the other side of the sofa, drawing in a coloring book.

"Hey," Lila says softly. Even a whisper sounds heavy here.

Mateo looks up. "Hey. Did you bring food?"

"Just leftovers." She glances toward the kitchen, wishing she'd brought something hot and filling. "I'll heat it up."

Their sister slowly looks up. "Can we have eggs tomorrow?"

Lila swallows hard, feeling guilty. She thinks about the empty fridge and how long it will be until payday. "Eggs tomorrow. I promise."

A quiet silence fills the room, except for the fridge's hum and a neighbor arguing on TV through the wall. Lila moves to the kitchen table and pulls the bills aside, scanning the dates and amounts that never seem to get smaller. The bills feel like a rising tide, threatening to take everything—heat, water, sleep.

Mateo pushes the book away. "Jennie gave me extra hours at the shop. If I work Saturday, I—"

"No," Lila stops him with a look. "School comes first."

He shrugs but looks tired and worried. "We need the money, Lila."

"We need you to graduate." Her voice breaks slightly. "You can't quit school to save us." She presses her fingers to her forehead, trying to push down her worry.

He stays quiet, holding his chemistry book tightly. "It's just.. . things are slipping, Lila. I missed practice. Missed the field trip. Mr. Greer says if I'm late again—"

"You won't be." She tries to sound sure, forcing hope until it feels fragile.

He looks away, his jaw tight. "I could just—"

"No." She stops his thoughts quickly. "I'll take more shifts. I can ask for extra pay. We'll manage, okay?" Her hand on his shoulder is both support and apology.

He nods, but doubt fills the room like the smell of burnt toast.

Lila moves to the kitchen, ready to heat dinner, her eyes burning. The light above casts thin shadows on the old floor as she leans on the chipped sink, her forehead almost touching the cold window. Her reflection shows pale, tired eyes and loose strands of dark hair. Outside, streetlights blur the rain into orange streaks.

Her thoughts spiral—she is always the one answering calls about bills, stretching cans of soup, deciding which bills can wait. She picks up shifts so the rent doesn't bounce. She remembers scraping together bus fare, letting her brother take the last clean jeans, even forging her mother's signature once so Mateo could go on a field trip. Each sacrifice leaves invisible scars.

She should fix this. She is the anchor, the last line keeping the world from falling apart. Asking for help feels like giving up, but with each bill on the table, with Mateo scared like an adult, and with her own energy drained from long shifts, she feels the ground slipping away.

For a moment, she imagines a different life—one where she leaves her hospital job, where dinners are warm and full, where laughter is common and they're not always near breaking. Freedom feels like a brief light before the dark—where even missing a paycheck means cold nights and empty cupboards. She wants to breathe but instead inhales worries.

Tears burn her eyes. She wipes them away before they fall and straightens up.

Turning off the kitchen light, she takes a deep breath of stale air and forces a practiced smile that says: It will be okay. Her feet carry her back to the living room, back to her family. The heavy choice waits inside her—a line she will soon have to cross.

Outside the glass window, the city glows with blurred neon and streetlights. Darius Hale stands still by the window, his body tight from years of control. His bare feet make no sound on the wood floor. He drinks whiskey, its smoky taste swallowed by the cold of the high-rise apartment. His reflection mixes with the city lights—the tight jaw, sweat on his temple despite the cold air.

Tonight, the outside world feels more real than his silent apartment. Traffic sounds mix with distant sirens, the city's pulse rising beyond the triple-glass windows. He focuses on the skyscraper lights, trying to drown out the voice inside that won't be quiet—a whisper from another life.

He turns away from the window, moving like a man stuck between two worlds. The apartment is quiet and empty, with pale walls and clean surfaces that feel cold. He moves to the desk and opens a drawer. Inside lies a small silver pin—the symbol of the Orion Brotherhood. It's sharp and heavy with meaning: a secret group bound by loyalty and blood.

He twirls the pin in his calloused hand, feeling its sharp points. Under his breath, he hears: "Love makes you reckless, brother. Choose wisely." The voice of Caius Drake, a warning. Darius tastes old whiskey and hidden truths.

Sitting down, he remembers the Brotherhood's secret meeting room—rich with wood and marble, where words became lifelong binds. He recalls tales of men destroyed by love: Martin disappeared after his lover exposed them; Silas lost everything after secret affairs forced intervention. Caius's own distant eyes warned of an unnamed danger. These stories taught one lesson—never let the world see who or what you love.

He traces the pin's edge, imagining the secret men at the table—willing to destroy even their friends to protect the group. Yet inside it all, loneliness grows: the cost of control is silence and cold nights. He thinks of a surgery's failure—flesh torn, hope lost, trust broken by his hands. This guilt never leaves him, driving his need for control. There is no room for weakness when one mistake can ruin lives.

Caius once said, love is a hidden crack that breaks the strongest bridge. Darius believed him. But then Lila's image appears—her hand on his arm after a crisis, her strength, her laugh that stirs something inside him he can't turn off. He tries to hide his feelings behind discipline but cannot. The more he thinks of her—the ink stains, tired eyes—the more his perfect life feels fragile and empty.

His throat tightens, breath shallow. He walks a fine line: between power and desire, secrets and truth, loyalty and hope that she might save him.

Fear pulses through him like a wild heartbeat. If the Brotherhood or hospital gossip finds out about them, Lila would be in danger, and he would lose everything—not just his place but the hope she gives him. Still, that fear is weaker than the pain of hiding who he is. If he dies a little every day, it will be because he never let anyone see him.

He puts the pin on the desk, shining under the lamp. His jaw hardens.

"Reckless," he whispers, a mix of challenge and truth.

Quiet except for the creaking chair, Darius walks down the hallway, shadows stretching along the floorboards, a locked door at the end. Fear and hope mix in him like electricity. Tonight, the world outside can burn if it must. He steps forward, heart beating fast but fragile, carrying the cost of loving Lila.

In the hospital hallway, bright lights press down as Lila opens the heavy lounge door. The hall behind her is empty and silent except for machines humming. Her ponytail loosens, hair sticking to sweaty skin. Her badge swings as she moves, the neat order falling apart.

Darius sits still at a worn metal table. Papers and scans are arranged neatly in front of him. His fingers tap a quiet rhythm on the edge of a file. The blue hospital light makes the room look cold and ghostly.

Lila closes the door behind her with a sharp click. The cold handle shocks her hand. She steps forward, rubber-soled shoes sticking to the tile. She stands across from him, the table between them like a barrier.

"I can't keep doing this, Darius." Her voice is low, shaking beneath the surface. "I'm thinking of leaving the hospital. I don't want to, but my family can't handle more. Mateo is disappearing under the stress. My sister missed two days of school last week because I wasn't there."

Darius doesn't react immediately. His calm doctor face shows no alarm. He fixates on a spot of dust on the table. When he finally looks up, his eyes betray nothing except a twitch in his jaw.

"Do you really want to leave? Or are you running from a choice you can't take back?" His voice is soft, barely heard. "Desperate choices can reveal everything we both—"

She interrupts, anger breaking through. "Reveal what, Darius? I'm open with you, and you hide behind riddles. Are you afraid of the hospital, the Brotherhood, or me? You talk about exposure like I'm a risk." Her hands run through her hair. "But you don't know what it's like to carry this alone. You warn me about consequences while my family falls apart. Do you want me to stay or just avoid the trouble?"

He raises his hands, trying to stay calm. "Lila, you know it's not that simple. You think control keeps me safe? I don't want this either. The Brotherhood—" His words catch. His cheek muscles tighten. "People here would destroy us both if they found out. I'm scared not just for me, but for you. For what could be used against you."

"Is that what scares you?" Her voice is raw. "Me? Or what you'll lose if it goes wrong?"

His eyes flicker, unsure. "Both."

Tension fills the room like two storms circling, close but not striking.

The light flickers uncertainly overhead. From the intercom, a garbled code sounds distant. Lila's arms fall, fists clenched from old anger. Darius's hand grips the table edge, knuckles white.

She looks at his watch and the scar on his hand. She fights the thought that she always reaches for something that slips away.

She thinks of home: crumbling walls, piles of bills, Mateo's tired smile stretched thin. Her mother's voice she imitates in tough times, stitched from memory and hope. The burden of fighting at work and home leaves her hollow. Facing Darius now, the weight is almost too much, but to give up on him means pain of a different kind.

They stand in rooms that feel like cages: his made of marble and glass; hers of debt and burden. He hides with silence and secrets; she holds tight to hope, even when it hurts.

Beneath unspoken fears, a darker fear beats—a fear of losing each other. Their fight is wounded by divided loyalties, but the bond remains unbroken, no matter how sharp their words. Her heart aches to trust—that Darius will choose her, that the Brotherhood is not always watching. She is tired of needing him to see her fully, scared they will always speak in codes and half-truths.

All that remains is silence. Lila turns to the door, tears welling but held back. Darius taps the table once, the sound hollow.

He stays seated. She stays. And between them, only hope remains fragile in the quiet.

The hospital lounge is quiet except for the vending machine's soft hum and flickering lights. Lila breathes in sharply, shoulders set. The air smells of antiseptic and burnt coffee. The room is hard: metal table, scuffed floor, blue light washing over Darius's tired face.

She faces him. A heavy feeling presses on her chest, but her voice is steady and strong. "I'm not leaving. Not unless you tell me to go. I'm tired, Darius. Tired of fear—fear of what might happen, fear of failing my family, fear of all this—deciding my fight." She looks at her hands, then back up, seeing flickers of feeling in his eyes. "If the Brotherhood, if the politics, if the walls close in—I will fight. But I need to know you want this too."

Darius doesn't move for a long moment. He is like frozen ice, tense as if a wrong word will break him. His hands tighten, then relax, resting on the table's edge, caught between keeping distance and needing closeness.

"I am..." His voice catches. He stands, trembling slightly, jaw working hard. "I'm scared, Lila." He runs a hand through his hair, looking younger, less firm. "Not just of the Brotherhood. Of you. Of losing you. Of what love might cost us. You're right. I've tried to control everything. I thought it would keep us safe—keep you safe." The words taste bitter, but he finally meets her eyes, his strength breaking. "But I can't keep you away. I need you. That scares me more than anything."

Silence falls, deep and delicate. The room feels smaller, walls filled with secrets. Hope presses hard against what could tear them apart. Lila steps closer, her hands shaking not from fear but relief. They stand on either side of the gap that kept them apart, hungry and distant.

Her hand moves forward, just touching his. Their fingers brush, careful—a new promise on the cold table. His hand is warm, rough, shaking. She meets his gaze; no words are needed: we face this together, no matter what.

Darius breathes in sharply and looks to the far wall. A small silver circle with the Orion Brotherhood emblem hangs near the door. His shoulders stiffen, eyes distant, as if the Brotherhood watches them. She feels his fear and anger. Even with their hands nearly joined, they are not alone.

Without words, she squeezes his hand, grounding them both. Her thumb moves over his knuckle. She can't promise safety or tomorrow, but she offers herself here and now.

They walk together to the door. The hallway beyond is dark and quiet, the edges dim and unsure—a place between worlds, hope mixed with fear. The hospital holds its breath for them.

In her mind, Lila's thoughts race through possibilities. If they survive tonight, what will come when enemies come knocking? She imagines Victoria Grant, cold and scheming; Dr. Crowe waiting to strike. Even friends could turn into threats if secrets leak—love and loyalty twisted by outside forces. What if one mistake destroys them? What will her family lose if the Brotherhood is crossed?

Still, deep inside, a stubborn hunger grows: she's tired of running. Maybe courage is always like this—rough, full of doubt, tied to impossible hope. Can two people hold back the tide? Or will betrayal break them, leaving their brief fight crushed by the Brotherhood's power?

Her heart offers no answers—only the certainty of Darius's hand in hers, footsteps in the quiet hall, and a promise glowing in the dark. Tonight, she will stand strong.

They leave the light and step into the uncertain dark together, their bond unspoken, their future unknown, but hope burning bright against the shadows.

Confession Under Rain

A razor wind sweeps rain sideways across the deserted courtyard, splattering half-moon arcs beneath the flicker of a jaundiced overhang. Darius Hale's shoes darken with each step as he paces, shoulders squared, his blazer wet from the waist down. The lights from St. Gabriel's windows throw long rectangles onto rain-washed flagstones, but the night consumes every edge, making the courtyard feel like an island cut off from the humming, antiseptic world of the hospital. Each time he draws breath, the cold stings his lungs; vapor ghosts from his lips. His hands remain buried deep in his coat pockets, knuckles aching from clenching around nothing.

He tries to count heartbeats—one, two, three—but the rhythm jumbles. That old ritual of control, a surgeon's steadying, fails him tonight. The roar of the storm drowns out every attempt at calm. Shadows creep in the periphery, twisted by the heady glow of the hospital's luminescence and the wild dancing of branches at the courtyard's edge. Every sound is amplified: rain pelting the metal overhang, the thump of blood in his ears, the near-imperceptible rattle in his breath when he can no longer keep it steady. He's waiting—not just for her, but for the words that won't stay locked inside any longer.

The service door creaks open, and a rectangle of harsher yellow light fractures the night. Lila Moreno steps through. Thin cotton scrubs are instantly drenched, clinging to every line of her body, her ponytail streaming against her neck, sneakers swallowing puddles. Rain beads along her jaw, drips from her paper badge, and soaks the skin at her throat. She doesn't hurry, doesn't flinch as water seeps down her spine and makes her shiver. She walks straight toward him—shoulders set, every step deliberate.

Darius watches, struck by her stubborn defiance of the storm. The world between them blurs: bars of rain cut them off from the hospital, and sound turns thick and muffled except for thunder. Lila's face is a study in determination, with no trace of hesitation as she pushes into the overhang's shadow. He sees the tremor in her jaw, the shimmer in her eyes—empathy cut with steel, a look no one else dares direct at him since the day everything fractured.

For a heartbeat, no one moves. Rain drums so loudly it masks the tremble in his chest. The weight building inside presses against the backs of his eyes and turns every muscle to lead. He can't keep the mask on, not now, not with her standing here, the storm shedding every external pretense.

His lips barely move at first. Words tumble out rough, unfamiliar on his tongue.

"I called you because I—" Darius hesitates, dropping his gaze, angling his shoulders away as if he might still retreat. "I can't run from it anymore. You asked what happened in OR 4. Why I... changed." He can hear the faint catch in his own voice above the rain, hating that it's there. "You were right. There was... a mistake. My mistake. One moment, and the world split open." His throat closes, guilt thick and sour, memory slick with panic.

"I lost a patient that night. I made the cut—a fraction too deep." He lifts a shaking hand, staring at his fingers as if expecting the blood to still be there. "Her heart stopped, and nothing brought her back. I was staring at my own hands—these hands that were supposed to be infallible." The words threaten to slip away, but he forces them out, one barb at a time. "One miscalculation, and I destroyed a life—shattered a family. All the Brotherhood's power, all my reputation... none of it could erase that stain."

Lila listens, silent but not passive. She closes the distance further, dripping footprints marking her passage. Darius feels the truth boiling up, sees her eyes fill with something that should be pity but isn't—not the kind that wounds, but the kind that makes his chest ache because it's real.

He forces a laugh, brittle as cracked ice. "Perfection. That's what they needed, what I was supposed to be. Untouchable. Efficient. The golden surgeon—Brotherhood's pride. But I lost myself in that room."

Rain pools at his feet, cold seeping through the soles of his shoes. Every sense is heightened: the ozone tang in the air, Lila's wet sandalwood scent beneath the hospital antiseptic, the way her breathing grows audible over the storm as she absorbs his confession.

He'd built so many walls, so many practiced silences. But here, where the world is reduced to rain and shadow, Darius lets the guilt show—lets it be raw and exposed. If she turns away now, he will let her. If she stays, he doesn't know what's left for him, but it will be real. For the first time in months, he wonders if the mask is finally breaking—if under all the shame, something worth saving remains.

Between them, the rain swells, a living thing that shields them from every watchful eye. Silence stretches, pulsing with the weight of what's been spoken. Darius stands, head bowed, words hanging between them—no shield, no pretense. The storm intensifies above; thunder cracks in the distance, mingling fear and anticipation until the night holds its breath, and neither of them moves.

They stand under the overhang, between rain and yellow lamplight, breath fogging in the wet, electric dark. The only sound is rain beating the concrete around them. Lila doesn't shiver. She holds his gaze, water running down her cheeks, and waits for him to continue.

Darius's hands are fists in his pockets. His jaw aches from clenching it too long, the storm's chill barely cutting through his tension. His voice is low, nearly drowned by thunder. "The Brotherhood—what they want—it's not human. If you bleed, you're weak. If you collapse, you're cast out."

Lila studies him, her hair slicked to her scalp by the rain, arms folding tighter across her chest. She is close enough for him to see droplets trembling on her lashes, glistening like tears. She waits, silent, refusing to let him retreat.

"I walk these halls every damn day," Darius says. "They watch everything. Every step, every breath is weighed. One wrong move and—" He stops, his voice faltering, forcing himself to look at her face instead of the ground. "After…the surgery…everyone looked at me like I was a wound that never closed. Not just a surgeon who failed—an imposter who never deserved to be here at all."

He presses his eyes shut, unable to bear her steady compassion. In his mind, the Brotherhood's code locks him in invisible shackles. Perfection or exile. It's all he's ever known, and it freezes him even as his bones shake from cold and shame.

The rain beats harder on the overhang, echoing in the silence that stretches between them. Lila steps in, her eyes bright with water—that is, and isn't, the rain. She doesn't hesitate; she reaches out, her hand searching for his under the sodden fabric of his jacket.

He doesn't want her to feel how badly he's trembling, but she finds his hand anyway. Her skin is cold, her grip fierce.

"You're not alone in this," Lila says softly. "You act like you're the only one who's ever broken. Like being perfect means you get to wall yourself off and carry everything on your own." She squeezes his hand, her thumb stroking the tight skin over his knuckles. "No one gets out whole, Darius. Perfection is a lie. Shame's a lie, too. You're not the only one bleeding."

He looks at her, rainwater dripping from his brow, lashes spiked with wet, his jaw slack with disbelief. Something hollows out inside him—a cave holding years of silence. She sees it all and doesn't flinch.

A heartbeat's hush—a shudder of wind, rain dancing in silver streams between them.

Darius leans in, searching her eyes for permission, for forgiveness, for anything at all. Lila doesn't look away. He lets himself fall.

Their mouths meet, desperate—soaked, raw, hungry. It's not gentle. Months roil between their lips: irritation, longing, nights spent pretending not to notice each other across stretchers and bloodstained sheets. Now all he can taste is her—rain on skin, warmth beneath the cold, salt, and the clean metallic tang of hope on her tongue.

Lila gasps into the kiss, fingers gripping the lapels of his coat, pulling him closer, pressing every inch of herself against him as if she could anchor him just by wanting to. The wind whips around them, carrying the sharp scent of ozone, the must of wet earth. His arms pin her in place, the world shrinking to the fevered heat where their bodies touch—rain-soaked uniforms, skin slippery and freezing, nerves burning bright as lightning.

Somewhere close by, the hum of hospital generators stutters under rolling thunder. It's distant, belonging to another universe. Here, the rain drums a cadence only they can hear.

Darius loses himself in her—the clatter of their teeth, the way her breath shakes, the small noises she makes when her hands slip under his collar and skim his bare neck. All the empty rooms inside him fill with her warmth, her insistence that he's not alone, that maybe he's not ruined beyond repair.

Lila's palm cups his cheek, her thumb brushing the faint scar beneath his eye. He sags, boneless with relief and exhaustion and craving. When he finally pulls away, he's panting, his forehead pressed to hers, their wet hair tangling, raindrops slipping down their cheeks like tears neither is willing to shed.

No words now. Only the wild sob of the storm, the pulse in his throat that hammers, reminders that he's living. That her arms—tight around him, grounding him—are real and necessary.

The distance between them is gone, scoured away by rain and revelation. For the first time, he lets her see all the shame and fear he's carried. She doesn't recoil. She only holds him harder.

In Darius, something stirs that's so strange he barely recognizes it—hope, sharp and unfamiliar, for a future with room for imperfection. Lila doesn't demand his secrets or force his wounds to close. She meets them, and him, with something fiercer than forgiveness—an acceptance that could remake everything.

In the shadowed court, cut by wet light and the muffled clamor of the hospital, they cling to each other. The rain catches in Darius's mouth as he tries to form words, but there's nothing left to say. Instead, he frames Lila's face with both hands, memorizing the heat of her, the rain-soaked skin under his thumbs, the answering pulse in her jaw.

He draws back just far enough to breathe, his forehead against hers, their noses brushing. Raindrops trace the space between their lips, their collected grief and want dissolving, just for an instant, into the wild, thundering dark.

Rain swallows the world beyond the courtyard, consuming even the far-off city lights, turning glass and steel into blurred smears of silver and charcoal. Water drums a low rhythm on the concrete, echoing in hollows and corners, a wild pulse that seals them against the world. A lone lamp, fixed above the overhang, flickers against the storm—its cone of buttery light slicing through where Darius stands, soaked to the skin, Lila pressed close. Their shadows entwine: two figures wreathed in rain and trembling possibility.

Darius draws away, just enough to see her—to really look. Lamplight dances over the angles of her cheeks, glistening on droplets that track along her jaw and collect at the hollow of her throat. Something in his chest eases, tight and aching. But relief tangles with terror, the two indistinguishable as thunder rolls off the hospital's eaves behind them.

"I never thought I'd get this," he says, his voice muted, nearly lost between the crash of rain and the distant wail of an ambulance slipping through slick city streets. "Not with all the ghosts I carry. Not with..." The word hangs, unsaid: Brotherhood. Every secret. Every misstep.

Lila's eyes shine in the half-light, unflinching, storm-bright and almost fierce. Rainwater gathers on her lashes, falling unheeded. She tilts her chin, draws breath, and for a long moment, doesn't speak. Only the tip of one hand trembles, nails digging into her own scrub shirt for warmth.

He wants to believe something fragile can still survive in this world: that hope can settle in the marrow, even here, even now. But the hospital's windows, fractured by rain, reflect a thousand watching eyes—judging, waiting for any sign of weakness. He shivers, not from the cold, but from the weight of everything that hunts him in the darkness.

"None of it matters if I'm with you," Lila says at last. "You think those shadows can claim what's ours? Let them try." Her voice is quiet, but her words are flint striking stone; there's defiance in the line of her mouth, and something fierce in the way she refuses to look away. Her hand finds his—still rough, still impossibly steady, even as it shakes.

"We've both lost things that can't be replaced," she murmurs, her thumb tracing the ridge of a scar across his palm. "But this? This is ours, Darius. The joy. The pain. No board. No secret handshake. No mask can take that from us."

He lets out a breath, ragged on the inhale. For the first time in months—a year, maybe longer—he feels the pressure inside him shift. Guilt doesn't vanish, but it's edged out by something luminous and raw. He closes his eyes, remembering the first time he walked these halls as a surgeon, every footfall heavy with ambition, with the weight of perfection perched breathless on his shoulder. Back then, there was always a voice promising that everything could be saved if he only tried hard enough.

But storms—real ones, secret ones—come for everyone.

Darius folds Lila's chilled hand in both of his and opens his eyes. "Then I swear to you," he says, his voice trembling, almost hoarse, "as long as there's breath in me, I'll fight for this. Even when it feels like the world's set on burning us down."

A half-smile slips across her face—tired, lit from within. "I know you will."

He wants to gather all the broken things, tuck them between the two of them so nothing else can get in. He wants to believe that redemption isn't a myth, that even men marked by failure and power can claw their way back to some kind of light.

She slips her arm around his waist, drawing him close until their sides are flush, her head settling into the hollow of his shoulder. Together, they press forward into the storm's hush, the rain softening every edge—the hospital's humming machinery, the neon fever of distant city traffic, the faint scuff of shoes against tile somewhere inside.

"I keep thinking about how fragile it all is," he finally says, barely more than a whisper against the storm. "How even the best moments feel like they might shatter. Sometimes I'm so afraid that I'll lose you before I even have the right to hold you."

Lila shifts, nudging her nose against his collarbone. "Maybe we will," she says, blunt as always, gentle as rain. "Or maybe we won't. But if I get another five minutes here, or fifty years, it's still worth it."

He nods, his forehead resting against hers, lips parted to hold in a thousand urgent promises.

Lightning flashes—brief and violent—throwing their entwined forms in stark silhouette across the slick pavement, as if the storm itself wants to remember this, to burn the memory of two souls defying the world's hunger for secrets. The thunder that follows rattles the hospital's glass, swallowing every doubt, every rule that should have kept them apart.

Side by side, they watch rain dance wildly in the lamplight, shoulders pressed as if they could hold the world together just by standing close. For now, the storm shelters rather than severs; for one lightning-lit heartbeat, hope feels like something real.

The night holds its breath. Wrapped in each other's arms, Darius and Lila face the darkness, clinging fiercely to the fragile warmth be-

tween them—alive in the eye of the storm, uncertain of what tomorrow might bring, unwilling to yield even a second of peace.

Love Exposed

Morning begins at St. Gabriel's Hospital with the smell of cleaning chemicals and the dull flicker of fluorescent lights on pale blue walls. The air feels heavy with tiredness and the quiet sounds of machines. Outside, a light rain blurs the city skyline. In the staff lounge, footsteps echo down the hall, a tired sound for the busy workers.

Emma Hayes stands by the coffee machine, holding a chipped mug, her eyes sharp under the steady lights. Near the door, she hears quiet voices—Darius Hale's, calm but tense, a warning she knows well; Lila Moreno's, softer but firm, not backing down. There's no kindness here: just quiet tension, an unspoken apology beneath the surface, shown in Lila's eyes, which reveal something deeper than anger. Darius's hand hangs uncertainly between them, then falls.

Emma tightens her grip on her mug and turns away, smelling burnt coffee. Secrets stick to the hospital's clean surfaces like dust, waiting for someone to uncover them. She's learned at St. Gabriel's that getting close to others brings power. Every argument overheard, every private look, can be used against someone.

At the nurses' station, Emma leans toward Regina Wallace. She lowers her voice to a whisper, loud enough to catch attention but soft enough to hide doubt. "Something's going on with Dr. Hale and Lila," she says. "They were arguing. Not about work." Regina raises her eyebrows, and the room stills; here, sharing news is an art, gossip is like painting pictures—Emma knows this, feeling her words slip away as others listen eagerly.

At St. Gabriel's, rank matters, but it's based more on how people are seen than on what they do. Saying the wrong thing can ruin a reputation. The Orion Brotherhood, a secret group, is always present—felt in how people avoid looking at certain men in the hallway and how the bosses ignore unfair acts, focusing only on top surgeons. Emma wonders if patients notice the fear that silence creates, the quiet power that moves through bedside talks and secret calls.

In the break room, the mood is tense, like electricity waiting to spark. Sofia Alvarez, sharp and always looking for a distraction, leans against the fridge, telling stories from bits of overheard moments.

"Do you know why Dr. Hale stays late?" Sofia says with a sly smile. "Think he's worried about paperwork? Maybe Lila is giving him special attention." Nurses laugh quietly. Someone mentions seeing Lila in the east wing after midnight; another says Darius was pacing near the stairs, looking tense. Stories grow: here, a glance is a secret, a smile is trouble.

"I heard her laughing near the private wing," someone adds. "Doesn't sound like work."

Sofia smiles, "Nobody spends that much time with Dr. Death unless there's something to gain." Nervous giggles spread around.

Later, as the shift changes, Lila enters triage, tired but alert to the eyes on her. Kate Jang, usually talkative, falls silent, fiddling with a patient chart. The air between them is quiet, stiff. Lila feels the weight of unasked questions; conversations stop as she comes near. Even the steady beeping of monitors seems louder.

Some nurses exchange looks, lips tight. One whispers, hand raised to hide words—Lila is invisible and impossible to ignore. Her skin itches under their stares, the meaning sharp and clear.

Emma stands nearby, feeling guilty. She didn't want to make things worse—just to share, maybe protect Lila if trouble came. But here, words change quickly, twisting the moment they are spoken.

Meanwhile, in the heart unit, Darius walks the shiny floors, tense. Dr. Harold Kim meets him, friendly in tone but with cold eyes.

"Careful, Dr. Hale. Rumors are spreading in the heart unit," Kim says lightly, meaning something more. "This hospital doesn't forgive easily." Darius stays quiet, jaw tight, pulse rising. Kim's words weigh on him; Darius knows what rumors can do.

The day feels long. Darius stops outside the operating room, his gloved hands on the glass. Inside, Lila moves calmly from station to station, caring for patients but hiding her inner turmoil. Nurses watch her with curiosity, suspicion, and jealousy. The harsh lights turn the hospital's white walls into a spotlight. Darius's presence feels like a lifeline—or a threat. The space between them trembles. Their private moments are broken, secrets leaking like stains on the floor.

Neither moves. The hospital waits, hungry for more.

The halls of St. Gabriel's hum with bright lights, every worn tile filled with tension. Lila breathes tightly as she enters the staff changing room, where old perfume mixes with the smell of clean sheets. Lockers stand like silent guards, worn by years of tired hands. She struggles with her locker lock, sweat sticking her scrubs to her wrists.

A white envelope is stuck between her uniforms—blank except for a faint fingerprint on the flap. A chill hits her chest. She tears it open, hands shaking. Inside is a note on plain paper, the message sharp: STAY AWAY FROM DARIUS OR SUFFER. YOU'RE NOT SAFE ANYMORE. The letters are pressed down hard, written to scare and warn clearly.

She sways, pressed between the cold locker and the flickering lights. Suddenly, she's eight years old again, hiding while her parents whispered about threats from a landlord. She wants to throw away the note, burn it, but can't. Her eyes dart around the room, to shadows behind a mop bucket, to her reflection in a bent locker door.

Her heart races as she heads back down the hallway. The staff lounge is almost empty—just some trash, the quiet buzz of a vending machine, and the soft clicking of sneakers. As she turns, footsteps sound behind her—fast and sharp. Julia Perkins appears, hospital badge swinging, smirking.

"Getting into habits?" Julia says softly, blocking her path.

Lila stiffens, squeezing the envelope tight. "I just finished my break."

"Right. Breaks with perks, huh?" Julia's eyes scan her, wanting a reaction. "They say some people here use favors to get ahead. You know—the unspoken rules."

"Don't talk about favors," Lila snaps, too fast. "You don't know—"

Julia sneers. "Think the Brotherhood or Dr. Hale will protect you if it goes wrong?" She taps the supply closet door quickly. "Not everyone gets away with breaking the rules. Just... remember who you are here."

Lila pushes past, knuckles white on the envelope. Julia's fake vanilla smell follows, like something rotten. The hospital feels too small now, every hallway tight, every look a question.

She finds Emma Hayes with medicine carts in the drug room. The smell of cleaning wipes and medicine is strong. Lila rushes in, puts the envelope on the table, her words spilling out.

"Emma, I found this in my locker." Her hands shake. "Then Julia trapped me. She accused me of trading favors for power. People whisper, but this is different. They're threatening me. What if they try to take my job? What if they go after Mateo—"

Emma frowns, taking Lila's hand firmly to calm her. "Lila, you're not alone. You've got me. We'll face this together." She looks at the note, lips tight. "Let them talk. I'll protect you. I promise."

"I can't lose this job, Em," Lila says quietly. "Not with Mateo. And now, it feels like no one is safe at work." She swallows, trying to steady her voice. "How do you fight a threat you can't see?"

Emma holds tighter. "You keep going. You don't let their poison get inside you."

Time passes slowly. Shift ends, and Lila leaves into the dark evening, city lights flickering on. The hospital looms behind, like an old shadow. On the bus, she keeps the envelope in her pocket, fingers touching it nervously.

Her apartment is small and smells faintly of spices and dust. She locks the door with three bolts, the clicks a small comfort. She walks past the sofa, shoes on, phone in hand, just listening—to her heartbeat, a neighbor's door closing, a message from Mateo lighting up the screen:

I'll be late. Don't wait up. Love you.

She sits on the worn couch, knees to chest. Julia's words loop in her mind—unspoken rules, remember who you are—while the letter's threat creeps under her skin. Being poor is one thing, but feeling powerless is worse. Now, she feels both.

Her life has been a struggle. She remembers her mother working night shifts, counting change so Mateo would get lunch. She learned to be strong, keep secrets, and stand firm. But tonight, her hands shake. She wonders when she will slip, when the whispers from the hospital halls will see how weak she really is.

She checks her phone for messages from Mateo and Emma. Shadows cross the floor. When headlights flash across the window, she ducks quickly, tight and ready. Her breath is fast and shallow; outside, the world is only passing cars and her own growing fear.

The envelope sits on the table, its white stark under yellow light. Lila doesn't know whom to trust. All she knows is that she, her brother, and even her secret feel exposed and vulnerable.

Sunset shines gold through the glass walls of the hospital's administrative wing, reflecting Darius Hale's tense shoulders as he stands outside Victoria Grant's office. Around him, the hum of elevators and soft clicks of footsteps fill the air. This hallway offers no safety; everything is too bright and sharp, and he feels eyes even when no one is there.

Victoria's office looks like a display of privilege: a neat wooden desk, glowing tablets, and a perfect orchid on a side table. Darius doesn't bother knocking—he enters with a calm that feels cold.

Victoria looks up, her face tight with thought. She takes off her glasses and presses her lips thin. "Dr. Hale, I guess this is not about supply issues."

"Rumors are hurting my team. I expect action." His voice is low and precise, but his fists are clenched.

She studies him carefully. "There's gossip every day. Why do you think I can stop every idle talk?"

"Enough." His voice cuts off, eyes sharp in the light. "This is serious—Lila Moreno is being targeted."

Victoria leans back, fingers joined. "What do you want me to do? I can't control every chat in the break room. Staff politics are tricky. If you want to avoid trouble, maybe you should remember where your loyalties lie, Dr. Hale. The hospital's reputation matters. So does the Brotherhood's."

He looks at her—a small scar near her brow, the quiet power behind her calm. She might fake sympathy if it helped her gain control, but tonight, she is cold. Darius leaves without another word, his shoes scraping lightly on the tile, anger burning.

He moves through the halls to the security office. The bright lights buzz around him, dulling the world. Inside, Chief Alan Thomas waits, a large man with arms crossed, eyes hard as stone.

"Dr. Hale," Alan says in a deep voice. "Not a usual visitor."

Darius skips formalities. "I need last night's footage. Cameras from stairwell three and nearby basements, from eleven p.m. to four a.m. Do it now."

Alan raises his eyebrows but opens the main screen, fingers moving fast. Monitors show grainy night views—the hospital quiet, corridors dark, rain blurring windows.

They watch. Footsteps echo, alone and soft. A nurse in pale scrubs looks nervous, hurries away. Another figure passes—a hooded jacket, head down, gloved hand steadying on the wall. Darius studies every move. He notes, records, just as the Brotherhood taught him: stay calm, watch closely, don't let feelings cloud judgment.

But he feels a tremble inside. The Brotherhood's rule is strict: protect secrets, sacrifice people if needed. No one is too important—not even him. Not even Lila, now a pawn in their secret fight.

"Pull facial data and cross-check," Darius says, his voice rough.

Alan nods. "I'll tell you if something stands out. But be careful—the wolves are close these days."

The screens flicker. Darius's reflection stares back, tired and empty, framed by false green light.

His office feels cold, no matter the rugs or soft lamp light. He stands at the window, hands on cold glass. City lights burn below, uncaring about the pain inside. He closes his eyes, remembers orders shouted in private rooms, Caius's voice like a command: Protect the Brotherhood at all costs. If a nurse or even a surgeon threatened to expose them, cut them out. Close ranks. No mercy, even when hands shake with regret.

Once, it was easy—he let the Brotherhood take over, discipline like armor against pain. But now that shield cracks, breaking whenever Lila's name is spoken in anger in these sterile halls.

He dials her before thinking, knuckles white on the phone. It rings once, twice, then she answers, breathless.

"Darius?"

"You need to be careful," he says quietly, mixing urgency with care. "Don't trust anyone you don't know. Don't walk to your car alone tonight."

A pause. A clatter—turning on a lamp, maybe dropping keys.

"Did something else happen?"

"I'm handling it. But things are getting worse." He sinks into his chair, runs a hand through trembling hair, guilt cutting deep. "I won't let anyone hurt you. I'm not leaving you alone, Lila. Not ever."

Her voice is soft, and for a moment, the hospital fades, leaving only her. "I trust you, Darius. Just... come home safe. Promise me."

He can't find words. The silence feels heavy.

When the call ends, he looks at the silent city. In his empty office, surrounded by polished quiet, he's caught between the Brotherhood's cold orders and the slow pain of love—knowing only one can win if the darkness inside St. Gabriel's demands a sacrifice.

Sacrifice

A cold wind pulls at Darius's coat as he steps out of the elevator. The city noise from twelve floors below is blocked by the thick walls of the penthouse office. Up here, the air feels different—heavier, with hints of new leather, polished wood, and a sharp smell like that before a storm. Dark glass windows show a mirrored city outside, hiding the real feelings of the people inside. Shadows shift around a shiny table, with unclear faces—just shapes in the soft golden light. The only color is a deep red silk handkerchief near Lucien Blackwell's untouched glass of whiskey.

There is a routine here, a careful order where no words are wasted. Darius knows these games well, but still feels a chill in his chest. The Brotherhood meets in silence, each man holding himself with old, careful control. They whisper and glance quickly—every move is noticed and remembered. At first, no one offers him a chair; they wait for Lucien to begin.

Lucien stands. The light catches the lines of his sharp jacket and the scar on his temple. His voice cuts through the quiet with firm control.

"We need you to listen, Darius. This is serious and final." He looks straight at him, his cold, deep eyes piercing. "You must cut all personal ties with Lila Moreno. Publicly and clearly. You cannot, under any circumstances, talk about Brotherhood matters to anyone outside this room—not to her, not to friends, not even in private. In return, you keep your job. Your reputation will be protected. Your place here stays safe." He pauses, letting the heavy price hang in the air.

Darius studies the scene: Lucien's hand resting firmly on the wooden table, other elders hidden in shadow. Power here doesn't need to be spoken; it's shown in the expensive watches and the quiet calm. Every window is a mirror, reflecting the city lights and the risks below.

An older man leans forward. His hands are smooth, but his voice is rough with age. "We have protected you and helped you become who you are. You know what will happen if you say no. We can ruin you with a single signature. One word, and your medical license will be taken away. You won't be the only one hurt. We have a long reach. Don't forget who we are or what we can undo."

His words hit like a sharp blade. Darius breathes in—clean air, but with a memory of blood. His knuckles turn white under the table as he forces himself to stay still. He moves his fingers, wishing for a scalpel, something real to hold; but all he has is silence and the heavy weight of knowing that love must be traded here, not kept close.

He looks at Lucien, then at the others—their faces unreadable, calm masks worn for decades, eyes that have seen reputations destroyed and lives ended. The Brotherhood's power is more than influence in offices or controlling news. It consumes secrets, controls desire, and traps its members in finely made cages.

On the outside, Darius hides his feelings. He touches his scar lightly, feeling its rough edge—a reminder of failure, of what happens when hands shake. He says nothing. He nods slightly, a quiet gesture filled with unsaid pain. The room changes. Lucien nods back; an elder presses a button, and a clock chimes, breaking the timeless feel with a cold sound.

The door opens silently. Darius steps away from the table, his shoulders stiff. He barely notices the men as he moves through the waiting room—the smells of cologne, cigars, and a sharp metallic scent from the security hidden in the building. Behind him, quiet voices start again, the power shifting with his silent answer.

He goes out to the balcony, the glass doors closing softly behind him. The city spreads below, a pattern of white, yellow, and red lights blinking through the fresh rain. The wind stings his face, easing the tension in his jaw but not the cold inside. He leans on the railing, his fingers raw on the wet metal.

Below, the city lives—car horns, distant laughter, life going on unaware. Up here, the Brotherhood's world tightens around those it owns. Each skyscraper shows their control; every reflected light warns what happens to those who fall.

For a moment, Darius thinks of Lila—not as a threat or a tool, but as the warm touch of her hand, her laughter that brightened dark days. He hurts, alone in the quiet space between worlds. Ahead lies a sharp choice—love on one side, survival on the other.

He stands up straight, his heart racing with a silent decision no man in that room could make him say tonight. Behind glass and shadows, the Brotherhood remains strong and untouchable. But out here, in the wind and city lights, Darius Hale is quietly starting to choose.

The city's quiet presses on him through the glass walls of Darius's apartment. The large room is dark but shines with neon light from outside. He closes the door softly. His coat falls from one arm, rain still beading on it, city dirt catching in the seams. He leaves it on a chair, pauses in the dim light, and breathes in the cold smell of expensive soap and steel. The only sound is his breathing and faint traffic far below.

He stands still in the clean, simple space. His reflection in the tall windows repeats—many tired men looking back. Memories rise: Caius's voice from long ago, the harsh rules of the Brotherhood, the sweat as he repeated their promises.

Brotherhood comes first. Family means nothing, friends mean nothing, love means nothing compared to loyalty to them. Sacrifice is the cost of power. If you fail, they take your heart before enemies can. Lucien's words cut sharply through his mind, still sharp after all this time. Caius had given those warnings in dim rooms, steady and firm—a warning shown in action, not just words.

He can still taste the metal from when he first had to watch a colleague be kicked out. The Brotherhood's way shaped him slowly: careful, cold, hard to read. Being perfect is the shield. Control is the weapon.

Now, the heavy price presses against his chest. They have given him an impossible choice: give up hope or lose everything, maybe even her. The city outside watches, lights and rain held still like a test.

He walks slowly, barefoot, the cold floor underfoot, while the world outside blurs. Sometimes he stops—shoulders tight, head down—waiting for steps that never come, a habit from years of fear. Over his desk, a folder lies open with hospital papers marked in red, heavy with meaning. He can almost hear Lucien: Serve us, or you are nothing. Perfect or dead.

But the perfection they want is a mask. He sees Lila now, as if she stands behind him—her laugh soft and warm, a kindness that calms frightened patients, brave when she touched the scar under his eye without pulling back. Her voice earlier in the hospital is sharp but brave, defending what she cares about even when danger is near.

He moves to the window, hands on the glass, city lights broken into sharp pieces. His throat tightens with words he cannot say out loud—not to the Brotherhood, not to Caius, only to Lila. She saw him fall apart: guilt entering behind the hospital door, hands stained with blood he could not clean, the memory of the operating room heavy with loss. She held him together then.

How can the Brotherhood tell someone to stop loving? How do you burn away a person who is part of you?

Suddenly, a quiet sound fills his mind—Lila's laugh over coffee; her whisper in the stairwell: "You don't have to be perfect with me. I see you." The first true comfort in years, breaking ice he had mistaken for strength.

He moves again, restless, hands clenching and unclenching. The past burns into the present: the failed surgery, the young life lost under his hands, the harsh judgment of failure. Every night since then, he rebuilt himself piece by piece, following the Brotherhood's rules. Tonight, seeing the city full of secret pain, he feels those rules cracking—maybe breaking beyond repair.

Behind him, the bed is messy—sheets tangled from restless nights. He sits at the edge, elbows on his knees, head bowed. For a long time, he lets grief hold him—a tie to memories both sweet and painful: how Lila's smell stayed on his shirt when she left, the silence she filled when her hand pressed to his chest, steadying him in chaos.

He looks up. His chest feels tight knowing what he must do before his mind says it. No more pretending. No more silence. No more hiding for men who gave him power but no mercy.

He will not give his heart away to them.

He stands slowly, as if in ceremony, shadow covering his face as he moves to the window. City lights pulse below, rain running down the glass like quiet tears. His hand rises, as if it could reach across concrete and memory to touch Lila's waiting palm.

Tonight, love, not the Brotherhood, will decide who he becomes.

Darius's thumb hovers over Lucien's name in his phone. The kitchen is dark, lit only by the city lights through tall windows, casting long shadows over shiny counters and quiet appliances. He calls. The answer comes fast, with no greetings.

"I want a meeting. Tonight. Face to face," Darius says. His voice breaks the silence.

There is a pause—a quiet tension like distant thunder. Finally, Lucien replies, calm but hard. "You will have it. The elders are waiting."

When Darius enters the Brotherhood's headquarters, the night is dark, rain misting the marble steps. The building is glass and black stone, rising like a sharp blade. Inside, the air smells like old leather and burned wood, mixed with something colder—a threat hidden as tradition.

The council room glows with soft golden light, a chandelier low, flickering across stern faces around a heavy wooden table. Old portraits watch from the walls, men with secrets and past victories in their eyes. Lucien sits at the head, flanked by Caius and other elders, their faces like stone. Darius stands at the door, coat over his arm, his heart beating fast in the cold quiet.

Lucien looks at him—cool and judging, but with a brittle edge now. "Dr. Hale. We expected your answer." His voice is soft, but the room feels smaller, every eye fixing on Darius.

Darius puts his coat on a chair and straightens, his mouth dry. Sweat pricks his palms, and dread fills him. Lila's laugh haunts the edge of his mind, warmth in the cold ambition.

He meets Lucien's eyes. "You told me to leave her. To erase everything we are. My answer is no."

A ripple passes among the elders. One, a thin man with white hair, leans forward, his voice sharp. "Do you know what defying us means, Dr. Hale? You risk not just your future, but hers too. The Brotherhood won't protect you. You both would be destroyed."

"My love is not yours to command," Darius says calmly, but his last word shakes slightly. Caius's eyes flicker—his concern turning dark. Around the table, hands tighten on armrests. Tension grows, near breaking.

"You think this is brave." Lucien's voice is smooth, but the threat is clear beneath. "One day, when they ruin her name and take your license—when whispers follow her family and your operating room empties—remember this moment. I'm giving you a choice: Brotherhood or exile." His words fall like a judge's gavel.

The air tastes sharp—fear, hope, betrayal. Darius clenches his jaw, forcing himself to hold steady. Inside, every lesson—the Brotherhood's harsh code taught since youth, scraped knees, years fighting to reach the top—clashes with the burning need to not disappear into the cold silence they offer. He thinks of Lila's hand in his, her quiet strength, how she never turned away from his scars or anger. What has the Brotherhood's loyalty meant if it's all about secrets and fear?

"Don't you see? This is not strength—it's decay. I won't let your tradition erase what's real. What's mine." His voice grows thick, but he keeps it steady.

Another elder, his voice low and cruel, cuts in: "You've been warned, boy. We can—and will—end you. Punishments worse than you know are waiting. The world forgets men like you when we want."

The threat is solid and cold. Panic scrabbles at Darius, but he pushes it down. He won't show weakness. His knuckles whiten. The power in this room, holding for centuries, feels less than complete—broken by the anger in his chest.

Caius looks at Lucien, a silent argument between old loyalty and harsh rules. Darius sees a flash of disappointment in his mentor's eyes, but also fear—fear for Darius or something bigger falling apart?

Lucien's voice softens now. "Walk away, Darius. Let this end quietly. You're turning yourself into a martyr for no reason."

"I don't want to be a martyr," Darius says, heat fading to dry calm. "But I'd rather be ruined than live by your rules, watching you destroy what I love to protect secrets you don't even believe in."

Lucien studies him, slow and long. "Courage, or blind recklessness?"

"Maybe both." Darius smiles faintly, almost a challenge. "But at least it's finally real."

He turns without waiting, picks up his coat, and walks from the room of judgment. His shoes echo on the marble floor. Behind him, the elders whisper—angry, tense, hurt in their own way. Darius hears glasses clinking and restless movements—men who cannot recall the last time a brother said no.

He closes the heavy, decorated door behind him. The hallway is silent except for a flash of lightning—brief bright light on black glass. Adrenaline shakes his veins, dread close behind every heartbeat. The Brotherhood's power is still there, but their hold on him finally cracks. For the first time, fear and relief stand side by side, charged by the storm.

Dawn light filters through St. Gabriel's big glass foyer, cold and blue. Darius walks the main hallway. There is a quiet hum under the fluorescent lights—the soft click of rubber soles on tile, the steady movement of staff. Voices near the nurses' station rise briefly, then fall silent as he passes. Their sharp eyes glance at him but look away too late.

Near the elevator, two surgeons wait, stethoscopes hanging from their necks. One mutters, "Did you see Blackwell last night? Word is Dr. Hale is finished," loud enough for Darius to hear. The other looks at him, then down. It is always the same—judgment mixed with doubt. The hospital itself feels like it's holding its breath.

He rounds a corner and smells disinfectant and copper—a morning drip behind a supply cart, the sharp smell scraping his senses raw. He's learned to move quietly, standing straight, taking less space than his tall frame really needs. Every step is controlled, as if precision could win back the respect lost to those who see him as a risk.

Upstairs, a quiet boardroom door closes. Inside, Victoria Grant sits at a large table, her eyes narrowed as she traces a folder with her finger. Two administrators lean close.

"You know what this means?" she says softly but sharply. "Dr. Hale's fall isn't just a scandal—it's a chance. Without Blackwell's support, the board will move against him."

One woman with sharp nails nods. "Should we leak the review of his credentials?" The other, unsure, smiles tightly.

Victoria's lips press tight. "No. We wait. The bigger the crack, the easier it is to step over. But keep the files close. One mistake, and we use everything."

Cracks spread through the shiny glass, invisible to those who don't see. Elsewhere, Lucien Blackwell meets the Brotherhood council in a bare conference room, old paintings dusty by the windows. The men stand quietly around Lucien. He holds a glass of water—untouched, still as the tension in the room.

Lucien's voice is cold and sharp. "He made his choice. If we allow disobedience now, tomorrow it will be rebellion."

The oldest man leans in, cuffs shining as his hands meet. "And if others feel the same as Dr. Hale, Lucien?"

Lucien does not blink. "Then we silence them all. The Brotherhood stays whole or it dies. Sacrifice is the only price we trust."

A soft sigh crosses the table. Uncertainty lies under every controlled move—no one wants blood on their hands, but no one wants weakness.

Darius heads to his office, feeling eyes watch him through glass and memory. He opens the door, and his screen lights up with a blinking alert: a message, so encrypted that it leaves no trace but fear. He opens it.

"We're watching. Choose your next patient carefully."

His phone vibrates at once. Sender: UNKNOWN.

"Your reputation won't survive another mistake. Neither will she."

Behind him, fluorescent lights hum. His palms sweat as he goes to his locker. Metal bangs as he forces the door open. A folded note slips out, precise and cold.

"You made your choice. Watch your back."

He stares at the paper, the same hands that hold a scalpel now shaking as if the world itself is uneven. Guilt lives inside him, twisting with resolve. The Brotherhood's punishment is not violence; it's erasing you. Your reputation fades, your skills are doubted, trust leaks away until only shadow remains.

He tucks the note in his pocket and pushes forward down the hall. Whispers of speculation follow him—his defiance, the surgeon brought low, questions of who will follow or betray him.

At the hall's end, light comes through glass walls, pale against storm clouds gathering over the city. Darius puts his hand on the glass, seeing his own blurred face. For years, control was his shield. Now, loneliness hollowed him, but something warm and stubborn is beating inside.

He opens his phone. For once, he drops caution.

"I won't let them break us."

He pauses just long enough to feel it—fear, hope, love's quiet fight—and then sends the message.

One floor below, in a dark break room, Lila's phone rings. She reads the words. Relief shakes her lips into a fierce, shaky smile, tears shining in her eyes as thunder rolls over the waking city.

Whispers of Rain

Rain hits the glass walls of St. Gabriel's Hospital, streaks of silver cutting through a cloudy gray sky. The city's tall buildings are hidden behind fog and rain. Above the sliding lobby doors, emergency lights flash quickly, casting a pale glow. Darius's shoes squeak on the tile floor as he walks in, his coat wet and cold. The smell of wet cloth mixes with the sharp scent of cleaning chemicals and the ozone from the storm outside. Hospital staff move quickly, checking charts and screens, speaking in low, urgent tones. Every action is sharp and careful—a plan to deal with a crisis—but their eyes are watchful and wary. Under the steady noise of machines and ringing phones, a tense feeling spreads—a quiet rumor moving like a heartbeat in the shadows.

The lobby, usually calm and orderly, feels shaken by the chaos. Lines break into small groups, and conversations scatter through the air, filled with secrets and quiet accusations over disposable coffee cups and the constant beep of monitors. Darius moves through the crowd, the uneasy mood swallowing even his usual calm. Nearby, a nurse leans toward a pharmacist, her voice unclear but her worry sharp. A young doctor nervously touches her stethoscope, glancing between a screen showing the weather alert and the hallway leading deeper into the hospital.

He walks down the staff hallway, taking each step with care. The storm presses against the building, thunder shaking the ceiling and lights flickering. Ahead, Dr. Sebastian Crowe and Victoria Grant walk together—calm and confident amid the chaos. Crowe's voice is low and serious, speaking just to Darius.

"It'd be a shame if another mistake ruins what you've worked for. Some reputations can't handle storms, Hale."

He leans in close, his cologne mixed with a clear threat. Darius meets his eyes and stays silent. Silence is protection here. Victoria's cold gaze and tight lips warn without words—you are alone and under threat.

They pass into a cluster of administrators. Darius feels their cold judgment follow him, sinking deep.

He turns a corner near the nurse's station, passing shelves full of patient files and rows of saline bags. Caius Drake appears, tall and quiet, his shadow stretching across the white walls. His dark eyes look sharply at Darius.

"Lucien is watching. The Brotherhood is impatient. They want proof of loyalty, now." Caius's voice is soft, almost lost in the rain's hiss. "One mistake, and you're out. Not just here. Everywhere."

Thunder crashes—the building shakes—and nearby, Lucien Blackwell stands with a small group of doctors. He smiles politely at a department head but never takes his eyes off Darius. It's a fixed, steady stare—calm but full of power. Darius feels it like heat on his back. Power doesn't have to yell; it waits, ready for weakness to show.

St. Gabriel's Hospital, a place built on order and clear rules, now feels full of fear. Hallways are filled with quiet guesses and suspicions. Every phone call seems to carry something dark—something not meant to be heard openly. Even the elevators seem slower, as if unwilling to carry the weight of whispered secrets. Inside these walls, agreements are made in secret notes and torn apart by careless words. Tonight, it's not medicine that rules, but secrets—a dangerous currency demanding payment with every heartbeat.

The hospital swallows Darius whole—cold and uncaring—but now alive with tight, unseen tensions controlled by the Brotherhood. He belongs everywhere and nowhere, his name whispered, his loyalty doubted. Inside, feelings pull at him: guilt like heavy bands on his ribs, memories of past mistakes always close, and pride—hurt and raw—burning beneath.

He wants forgiveness, badly—a way to clean the marks on his hands. He wants to run, too, but love makes things complicated. Lila's presence is a lifeline in the future he imagines with every step. The cost to keep her safe, to hold onto hope, grows along with the storm outside.

Lila crosses the lobby, her dark hair pulled back, scrubs sticking damp to her. She doesn't hesitate when she reaches him—her hand closes over his, steady and sure. Her thumb traces the scar under his glove. Her dark, strong eyes meet his.

He takes comfort in her, letting the tension settle in his throat and shoulders, but she keeps her gaze. The lobby, the busy staff, the tense power struggle all fade away. In her grip, he feels human—shaking but understood.

"Whatever happens," her squeeze promises, "I'm here."

Lightning flashes. Thunder rolls through the glass, shaking coins in his pocket and rattling monitors. The storm outside echoes the violence inside the hospital. Darius and Lila hold each other's eyes as the building shakes around them—caught in the center of the coming storm.

The fluorescent lights buzz and flicker as rain leaks in under the door with each new arrival. The main boardroom at St. Gabriel's is thick with the damp smell of wet clothes, umbrellas, and hidden worry behind formal faces. Department heads, Brotherhood elders, and board members sit around a shiny wooden table. Rain-dark coats drip onto the floor. Their faces are tired and watchful. Eyes avoid each other, full of suspicion, secrets, and silent blame.

Darius stands at the table's head, shoulders stiff, his reflection broken on the shiny surface. Every breath tastes of disinfectant and disaster. Thunder crashes outside, but the tension here is heavier on him. To his left, Lucien Blackwell keeps his hands folded over a sealed ledger; Caius Drake sits to his right, calm but with nerves showing.

Everyone stops talking when he speaks. "I have proof," Darius says quietly but firmly, his words clear and commanding. He opens a file. Pages spread out, emails shown on frosted glass screens, time-stamped schedules marked with changes. The hospital's records, once perfect, now show signs of betrayal, clear and damning.

He names names. "Dr. Crowe. Ms. Grant." Gasps ripple around the table. Victoria sits up straight, her green eyes sharp and calculating. Sebastian's jaw tightens, glaring at the folder as if he can burn it with his eyes. Documents move around—changed schedules, fake nursing reports, missing notes, orders confused. Patient safety was put at risk, all during the nights tied to Darius and Lila.

The storm outside grows louder, hitting the windows hard, matching the unrest in the room. Caius's face is serious and grim. Lucien leans forward, his every action showing how serious the accusations are. The Brotherhood watches, both protector and judge.

Sebastian loses his temper. He stands, shouting against the tight, humid air. "This is a lie. You're desperate, Dr. Hale. You'd sink anyone to save yourself."

Darius does not back down. "There's a timeline. Ask anyone here who signed the night logs—who changed orders without reason, who moved staff from my cases." His eyes scan the room, looking for courage in faces beaten down by rules and fear.

Silence stretches. Then a young doctor, pale and tense, speaks. "I remember. I was told to follow new post-op orders but didn't see the original. It felt wrong." His voice shakes, but the dam breaks. Three nurses and two more doctors nod, tired but truthful. Loyalty cracks; whispers turn heavy with truth after years of self-preservation.

Victoria meets Lucien's eyes. A flash of annoyance and fear, then resolve. She crosses her arms, lips tight, quietly watching.

The Brotherhood members shift, half angry, half shocked. Lucien finally breaks the silence. "We will have order." His voice leaves no room for argument, sharp from years in the shadows. He looks sharply at Darius and Sebastian—a mix of warning and judgment.

Darius feels a clear strength beyond fear. The Brotherhood's rules protect, but they also trap. Caius's steady eyes silently beg Darius to be careful, to protect the Brotherhood first. Lucien, always a strategist, calculates the cost.

Darius's jaw tightens. He turns away from their customs. "If loyalty means silence while corruption grows," he says, "I refuse. No more secrets if it risks Lila, our staff, or patients."

The room erupts. Hands slam, voices rise, chairs scrape. The hospital director tries to calm things but is drowned out by shouting. Sebastian yells, losing control, while another doctor approaches angrily. Security rushes in. The noise is chaos—accusations, fear, and outrage.

Lila's heartbeat races beneath the noise, her face pale but eyes fierce as she looks at Darius, pride and fear mixed.

He grabs her hand under the table, steadying them both as the storm rattles the old windows. "I choose truth over silence," he says, not just to the room or the Brotherhood, but to her. "I choose her."

Lightning lights the rain curtain. Voices fill the space. Two worlds—the hospital and the secret Brotherhood—clash in the storm's reflection. In that moment, lines of loyalty and love are redrawn, and the future balances on the edge of rebellion and consequence.

In St. Gabriel's halls, the storm leaves only wet marks on glass and a quiet that replaces the usual noise. People talk quietly in small groups near the nurse's station and under cold, blue lights. Some nurses shrink away and glance at Darius nervously, still shaken by the boardroom fight. Others, braver or too tired to hide, whisper support or look at him with a mix of defiance and hope.

Without meaning to, Darius becomes a new force in these halls: someone crossing the dividing lines. The floors, once shining and neat, feel full of doubt and worry. Still, a quiet tension fills every breath. The rustle of uniforms and the sharp smell of cleaning chemicals are stronger than usual. The air feels different—sharper, alive with rain hitting the roof and the rush of adrenaline, half fear and half hope.

Emma appears near Lila, moving quickly through the nervous crowd. She hugs Lila tightly for a moment.

"You shook things up, Moreno. Bravery spreads, you know." Her voice is soft but clear, and a few nurses nearby smile a little.

Lila relaxes for a moment. She grips Emma's sleeve hard. "It wasn't just me. No one stands alone anymore."

Emma nods fiercely, and the feeling spreads. People straighten, and junior staff move closer. Lila watches, eyes bright, as the quiet turns less hostile—softened by hope that maybe these cracks can heal.

Darius, finally breathing clean air, leaves the boardroom. The doors close quietly behind him. He feels empty and tense, every sense sharp—the scrape of his shoes, the sweat on his collar, the fading rumble of thunder outside. Caius stands at the window, arms crossed, framed by pale light. Their eyes meet, and with a small nod, they share rough respect and tired acceptance. It's a small gesture but filled with meaning: the Brotherhood's shield is still there, battered but alive.

A young surgeon approaches nervously, like stepping on thin ice. "Dr. Hale. Thank you. For..." His voice falters, but he continues, looking past Darius. "For letting us matter."

Darius responds quietly, barely moving—a slow blink breaking his usual calm. He doesn't reach out or smile. But as he moves on, his face softens—a crack in his hard shell. After years of solitude, he allows a quiet gratitude. This unspoken moment promises a new way forward.

He finds Lila waiting at the far hall. Neither speaks at first. Their fingers find each other, palms pressed together as if making sure the other is real and still there.

"You're shaking," Lila whispers.

"So are you," Darius says honestly. The need to be perfect is gone; it's enough to just be with her.

Together, they open the doors to the ambulance bay. The rain slows to soft taps on tarps and concrete. The world smells of wet earth and ozone, mixed with the hospital's sharp scent. Outside, the city blurs in rain and mist, lights smeared like a watercolor. The chaos inside seems very far away now.

Lila leans against him, her cheek resting on his damp shirt. Her breath is warm on his chest, their hearts beating fast with feelings too deep for words. The tiredness sticks to them, but in the quiet after the storm, there is a closeness sharper than any words.

"If you need to run, now's your chance," Lila says, a teasing sparkle in her eyes. She is braver now, her fear changed by surviving the chaos.

He shakes his head, his hand lifting to cup her jaw. "I've spent too much of my life running. We face storms. We survive. Sometimes, we even... change."

She laughs, tired, tears in her eyes. "The world didn't end. But it won't ever be the same, right?"

"No," Darius answers quietly. "But maybe we don't want it to be."

They stand in stillness, arms wrapped around each other—fragile but unbreakable. Behind them, hospital lights flicker as staff keep working, voices rising and falling, normal life moving forward on changed ground. For the first time in days, there is something like hope. Lila closes her eyes, resting her forehead against Darius's chest as the world outside finally goes on.

The Brotherhood's private dining room is quiet, lit by soft golden light from chandeliers reflecting off the shiny wood and showing tired faces. The table looks ready for a ceremony, but plates are untouched and silverware rests silent on cloth napkins. Shadows fill the corners, spreading across portraits of past leaders whose painted eyes seem to watch the men now carrying their name.

Darius sits stiffly, elbows on the table, hands steepled in front of him. Rain softly taps the tall windows. The air smells of leather and leftover spices from food not eaten. Caius's shoulders droop, a rare weakness in his strong frame. His eyes flick to the empty chair next to Darius, then back with a quiet look. Lucien sits with arms crossed, still as a statue, but his dark eyes watch every small move.

Silence stretches, fragile as glass. Darius breathes in, feeling tightness deep in his chest and thunder echoing through his bones. He is no longer the man they once praised—a surgeon shaped by strict rules and the Brotherhood—but something raw, still burning with defiance.

"My loyalty isn't to silence," Darius says, his voice sharp but not cold. "Not anymore. It's to Lila. To the truth, if that saves even one innocent person from being hurt by this—by us. Whatever the cost, I'll bear it. I don't care who tries to take away what's left of my name."

Caius closes his eyes, then opens them, sliding a glass of amber liquid across the table. The glass shakes slightly, but his hand is steady. "You know what you're risking. Burn one bridge, and the whole city can catch fire. Makes a man wonder if his belief is worth the ashes."

Lucien straightens, fingers tense. "Is that what you want, Darius? To burn down everything we built—loyalty traded for a woman's love and a moment of pride?" His voice cuts, but without anger—only tired seriousness. "Or is this something more?"

Darius turns the glass in his hand, ice clinking. "This is the only way the Brotherhood will survive. You know that, Lucien. The world is already watching. If we don't change, we're finished—just ghosts behind glass, pretending secrets protect us when they only bring fear."

Caius smirks, part pride, part sadness. "You take after your father—always did. He would have fought for what he believed. Looks like you will too."

The air tightens, full of things left unsaid. Thunderlight flickers on Lucien's face, making his eyes look empty. "Change comes for us all. But be warned, Darius—enemies are watching who know our faults. The higher you climb to fight the rot, the more you're in their sights."

Darius watches these men—brothers not by blood but by the sins they share—and wonders how many eyes are watching, waiting for a chance to break the walls they built. He imagines boardrooms lit in cold blue, rival doctors making secret deals, old money and new tech dancing a hidden dance. It's not paranoia; it's knowing that every open move draws powerful enemies who want to tear them down. Tonight, the game changes—lines drawn, alliances shifted. By choosing Lila over silence, has he made them untouchable or just put targets on their backs?

Still, a fragile hope beats in Darius's chest. Maybe this break is the first breath of something better. If he's learned anything, it's that silence hurts deeper than truth.

Footsteps come softly on thick carpet. Gold light catches Lila's eyes as she enters, Emma just behind her. Their energy shakes the men's quiet power. Lila moves beside Darius; he takes her hand, their fingers locking tightly. Her knuckles are white, but her stance is strong. Her look to Caius and Lucien says clearly: You haven't broken us.

Emma stands by Lila, not shrinking before the old Brotherhood's power, chin high, eyes steady. In the silence, the line between old ways and new is not erased, but crossed on purpose.

Lightning flashes outside, branches of white light across the dark city sky. Lucien glances toward the window. For a moment, their reflections show on the glass—united, fragile, glowing in a storm that has only paused.

"What we've started tonight will bring out our enemies," Lucien says softly, only to the group. "None of us can stand alone when the real storm comes."

Epilogue

The rain had stopped.

For the first time in years, Darius stood beneath a quiet sky, his hand wrapped around the one that had taught him how to breathe again. The city glistened with reflections, every droplet carrying away pieces of the man he used to be. He wasn't whole—not yet—but he was no longer afraid of the storm inside him.

As he looked at her, he realized healing didn't mean erasing the past. It meant choosing love, even when the shadows whispered otherwise.

A faint vibration from his phone broke the stillness. The name flashing across the screen made his mouth tighten in both irritation and amusement.

Orion Vega.

The reckless one. The storm Darius had never been able to predict. If there was trouble in the world, Orion found it—or built it himself. His message was short, but telling:

"They're watching me. And this time, I may not walk away. Meet me."

Darius slipped the phone back into his pocket, his gaze drifting toward the skyline where Vega's empire of glass and steel towered, both magnificent and fragile. He knew that tone in Orion's words. It was the sound of a man spiraling—of desire and destruction chasing each other like lightning.

Darius tightened his hold on the woman beside him. Somewhere, in another corner of the Brotherhood, another life was about to unravel.

And when the storm broke, it would not whisper like rain—
it would roar.

Final Thoughts

When the last chapter closes, it isn't just a story of a surgeon and the woman who unraveled him. It is a reminder—that even the strongest hands tremble, even the most guarded hearts bleed, and even in the fiercest storm, love finds its way through.

Darius Hale's whispers are not just about loss. They are about renewal. They are about remembering that healing is not forgetting, but daring to begin again, even when the past still aches.

To you, dear reader: if you have carried storms within, may you know that you are not alone. May you believe, as Darius learns to believe, that brokenness can still be beautiful, and that rain can carry both sorrow and hope.

But the Brotherhood's story is far from over.
The shadows gather. The ties that bind these men will soon demand more than passion, more than sacrifice.

And as you close this book, know this—
the rain was only the beginning.

Review Request

LOVED the Orion Dynasty Book Series?

<u>Click here to leave your review on Amazon.</u>

Your review helps this dark billionaire romance world reach new readers who crave power, passion, and redemption.

Or type this link into your browser:

https://www.amazon.com/review/create-review?asin= B0FSKF8DVD